∾ THE TAILS OF FREDERICK AND ISHBU ∾

The Mystery of the Burmese Bandicoot

Marshall Cavendish Corporation
99 White Plains Road
Tarrytown, NY 10591
www.marshallcavendish.us/kids

The following quotes which appear in this book are in the public domain:
p. 4 from "To Althea, from Prison" by Richard Lovelace
p. 7 from *The Merchant of Venice* by William Shakespeare
p. 83 from "Poem of Joys" in *Leaves of Grass* by Walt Whitman
p. 133 from "The Rime of the Ancient Mariner" by Samuel Taylor Coleridge
p. 140 from "Sea-Fever" by John Masefield
p. 197 from "The Bard: A Pindaric Ode" by Thomas Gray
p. 241 from "Requiem" by Robert Louis Stevenson

Library of Congress Cataloging-in-Publication Data
Cox, Judy.
 The Mystery of the Burmese Bandicoot / by Judy Cox ; illustrated by Omar Rayyan. — 1st ed.
    p. cm. — (Tails of Frederick and Ishbu)
 Summary: Two rats escape from their comfortable life in an elementary school classroom and survive many dangerous adventures as they stow away on a pirate ship in search of a valuable statue.
 ISBN 978-0-7614-5376-5
 [1. Adventure and adventurers—Fiction. 2. Rats—Fiction. 3. Mystery and detective stories.] I. Rayyan, Omar, ill. II. Title. III. Series.
 PZ7.C83835Bur 2007
 [Fic]—dc22
 2006102917

The text of this book is set in Spectrum MT.
Editor: Robin Benjamin
Book design by Vera Soki

Printed in China
First edition
10 9 8 7 6 5 4 3 2 1
Ⅲ℃ Marshall Cavendish

To the fifth-grade class next door at Pioneer Elementary,
and to the kindergartners at Willamette Primary
who heard the story first,
thanks for the help and inspiration

∞

∞ THE TAILS OF FREDERICK AND ISHBU ∞

The Mystery of the Burmese Bandicoot

by **Judy Cox**

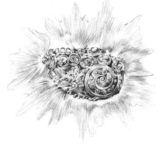

with illustrations by
Omar Rayyan

Marshall Cavendish

∽ CONTENTS ∽

Prologue:
THE CAGE DOOR OPENS

Stone walls do not a prison make,
Nor iron bars a cage.
—Richard Lovelace

THIS IS THE TALE OF TWO RATS, FREDERICK AND HIS BROTHER, Ishbu, who lived in a cage in Miss Dove's fifth-grade classroom.

One day Millicent Mallory left the cage door open, and the rest is history. Frederick (that's the brave rat) saw his chance. He scampered right out. At first Ishbu (he's the timid one) refused to go, but a sharp nip on the ankle from Frederick persuaded him.

Once they were both out of the cage, they darted down the heater vent in the floor and slipped into the duct, which to them was just another small tunnel. Rats like tunnels very much. They find small, dark places irresistible. In fact, Ishbu was so comfortable that he wanted to stay there, but

Frederick had a different plan.

"Come on, Ishbu!" he hissed. "Don't stop now!" And so they went on, down the twisty corridors and up the narrow passageways deep in the old school. And finally even Ishbu saw the light at the end of the tunnel.

It was the boiler room window. Frederick wriggled out and looked around. Ishbu crawled out and looked at Frederick.

The boiler room was a dank, narrow little spot, lit only by a tiny window high in the wall. Fortunately for the rats the window was open just a tad. Frederick sniffed the fresh outside air and scrambled up the rough brick wall, using the hollows in the crumbling mortar as toeholds. Ishbu, who didn't want to be left behind, followed. They paused on the windowsill and stared out into the dull, rainy winter day. . . .

Part One: LAND

There be land-rats and water-rats,
water-thieves and land-thieves . . .
                        —William Shakespeare

A HARD, COLD WORLD

 FREDERICK WRIGGLED OUT OF the partly opened boiler room window. He was a gray rat with shiny black eyes. Rats that particular color are called lilac. It doesn't make sense, really. Lilac is usually a shade of purple, but Frederick was pale gray.

He had a skinny pink tail. The fact that it was hairless might have been a bit alarming; but if you were to pick up Frederick, his tail would curl around your wrist in a most appealing manner, like a friendly garter snake.

He was athletic and trim, due to all the laps he'd run on the hamster wheel of the cage in Miss Dove's fifth-grade classroom. He dropped nimbly down from the windowsill to the ground below, landing gracefully on all four feet.

Ishbu was not so lucky. Ishbu was a hooded rat:

his body was white, but his head and shoulders were black. Like Frederick, he had sharp teeth and claws, and a pink hairless tail. His eyes were also black. But Ishbu was a bit on the chubby side, preferring naps to running laps and leftover birthday cupcake frosting to a diet of nuts and carrot sticks. He puffed and huffed as he tried to squeeze through the narrow opening. At last he squirmed through. He clung to the window ledge and stared down at Frederick.

"Jump!" Frederick called.

Ishbu didn't answer. He trembled as he gazed at the ground so far beneath him. *I'm a million miles up,* he thought. *So high, the humans look like ants. Oh, wait. Those are ants.*

"Hurry, before Millicent discovers we are gone and comes to look for us!" urged Frederick.

"Freddy, I'm scared," whimpered Ishbu. "I can't do it. I can't. Don't make me. Let's go back." A cold dollop of rain dripped from the top of the window frame and ran down Ishbu's back. "At least our cage was warm and dry. And we had three meals a day." His whiskers quivered. "Plus snacks," he added with a sniff.

Frederick looked up at Ishbu and shook his head impatiently. "Sorry, brother. But I've got to do it."

He climbed easily back up the crumbling brick wall and nipped Ishbu on the paw. Surprised, Ishbu let go of the ledge and tumbled to the ground. He turned a complete somersault and landed on his back. Frederick dropped down next to him.

The day was cold and raw, but the smell of freedom was in the air. The two rat brothers lifted their wiry whiskers to the pale sunlight filtering through the clouds. A sense of adventure as sharp as a knife spurred on Frederick, but a feeling of doom dampened Ishbu's spirits.

There was no time to linger. Daylight hours are not safe for small nighttime creatures, no matter how brave, no matter how cowardly. Rats have many enemies: hawks, eagles, ferrets, cats, dogs, wolves, lions, tigers, alligators, and coyotes; humans with brooms, traps, and poison; and little kids with BB guns.

It's a hard, cold world out there. Especially when you are only six inches long and weigh less than a pound. Frederick and Ishbu didn't know what lay ahead of them. But they knew one thing— they needed to hide as soon as possible.

Side by side they dashed for the bushes clustered at the edge of the playground. Safety meant a hole, any kind of hole—a culvert, a gully, a tunnel, or a burrow. Any port in a storm, any pot in a pickle, any jar in a jam . . .

They crossed the open playground, Frederick racing along easily, Ishbu panting and sweating. Just before they reached the shelter of the shrubs, a dark

shadow passed over them. Rats can see in all directions. That's the advantage of having eyes that stick
out like shiny round beads. They saw the shadow
overhead and immediately had the same thought:
danger! Then they did what most small animals do
in the face of peril. They *froze*.

Curious but true. Perhaps the prey thinks the
predator won't see it. Sometimes it must work. But
in this case, Ishbu's white fur and Frederick's lilac
coat were quite easy to spot against the dark, damp
asphalt of the playground.

MILLICENT MALLORY

Why were Frederick and Ishbu so desperate to escape Miss Dove's classroom that they were willing to risk their lives? It was not merely the call of adventure that lured them out on the fateful day Millicent Mallory left the cage door open—although Frederick *did* yearn for adventure, especially after hearing Miss Dove's stories of explorers, heroes, and travelers.

No! It was Millicent Mallory herself who forced Frederick to flee. And now it was the fear of Millicent that froze Frederick and Ishbu as the shadow darkened the sky above them.

∞

Only an hour ago Ishbu was napping, as usual, on the third floor of their multilevel wire rat cage. He'd eaten his fill of sunflower seeds, and besides, daylight always made him sleepy. He curled up like a

12

cat, with his tail over his nose. His chest rose and fell, fell and rose; and from time to time he smacked his lips. He dreamed of food.

Frederick, on the other hand, was wide awake on the first floor. He pressed against the bars, eyes bright and shiny, ears pricked, whiskers vibrating. He listened so intently, he scarcely breathed. Miss Dove was teaching *geography*.

Of all the subjects the fifth graders studied, geography was Frederick's passion. He loved the maps, globes, atlases, and charts Miss Dove used. He loved to listen to her stories of far-off lands. He dreamed of Lapland and Australia, of penguins in Antarctica, of palm trees in Borneo—*faraway places with strange-sounding names.*

Just then Miss Dove was teaching a lesson on latitude and longitude. Frederick watched carefully as she drew on the chalkboard.

"This is called a compass rose," Miss Dove said in her sweet, gentle voice. She pointed to the compass symbol. "It looks like the petals of a flower, doesn't it?"

The class yawned, but Frederick leaned forward and nodded, his nose twitching.

"North, East, South, and West," continued Miss Dove. "Those are the directions on the compass. Here's how to remember them—Never Eat Soggy Worms. The first letter stands for each direction."

"Never Eat Soggy Worms," repeated Frederick dreamily. "How clever!"

Meanwhile, on the other side of the classroom, Millicent Mallory poked Jason Gumm with her pencil. She liked to do this. She was a big, round girl with eyes like gooseberries. She wore her pale, carrot-tinted hair in two limp braids. Jason Gumm was a little, scrawny boy. His nose was always dripping. He didn't like to be poked with a sharp pencil—who does?—but he was afraid to tell on her. Most of the children in Miss Dove's class were afraid to tell on Millicent Mallory.

"You're a genius, Millicent," whispered Kay Serah. Kay thought everything Millicent did was brilliant. She hid her grin behind her atlas. (She did this because she seldom brushed her teeth, and consequently they were the color of old piano keys.) A skinny girl, Kay had a nose as pointy as an ice pick. Dark hair hung around her face in lank tendrils.

"Millicent! Kay!" said Miss Dove sharply. "Turn around, girls. Pay attention. You need to know this."

"When will we ever need to know this?" grumbled Millicent, but she turned around. Under her desk she snapped the lead point off her pencil. Then she put the pencil on her desk, folded her hands on top, and smiled sweetly—as if that would fool anyone.

Frederick didn't see any of this. He already knew

what a bully Millicent was. Most of the time it was best to ignore her. He concentrated on Miss Dove. Today she wore a lilac sweater (his color!) with a bunch of violets pinned to the collar. She pulled down the world map and pointed at it with a yardstick. Frederick couldn't wait to hear what she'd say next.

"Now, children. Longitude goes the *long* way. Latitude goes the *short* way. Picture a fat man wearing a belt. The equator is like a belt around Earth. Remember *lat* means *fat*, and you'll always know that latitude goes around."

Millicent raised her hand.

Miss Dove sighed and put down her yardstick. "Yes, Millicent? What is it now?"

"My pencil broke. Can I sharpen it?"

Miss Dove reluctantly nodded.

The pencil sharpener hung in the back of the classroom, next to the table with the rat cage. Millicent walked down the aisle, jabbing Jason once more, just for practice. At the sharpener, she took her time, grinding her pencil to a long, lethal point.

Frederick continued to ignore her. Miss Dove went on. "Lines of longitude go up and down Earth, like the segments of a peeled orange."

But the noise of the pencil sharpener woke Ishbu. He ran down the ramp to the bottom of the cage, his nose twitching. "Hey, Freddy," he called. "Is it lunchtime yet?"

Now, although Millicent was close by, she wasn't alarmed by a speaking rat for one simple reason: Frederick and Ishbu understood English, but they spoke Animal. In addition to squeaks and snarls, growls, purrs, grunts, mews, and teeth clicking, Animal also uses silent signals, such as tail positions, whisker twitches, eye blinks, ear swivels, and scratches, as well as odors. So Frederick and Ishbu could carry on long, deep, philosophical discussions (although Ishbu usually wanted to talk about food), and all humans would hear were a few squeaks.

Millicent didn't know what Ishbu was saying, but his movement caught her eye. She put down her pencil and glanced at the front of the room, where Miss Dove still pointed to the map. Millicent smiled again, and this time it wasn't a sweet smile at all. She opened the cage door and grabbed Ishbu by the tail.

Millicent pulled Ishbu out of his cage and dangled him upside down. He squirmed and wiggled but couldn't get free. Kay turned around in her seat, hiding her grin with her hand. This was like applause to Millicent Mallory. She swung Ishbu back and forth. The pain in his tail was excruciating. Millicent picked up her pencil and was about to poke him in the belly with it. . . .

"Freddy!" cried Ishbu. "Help!"

Without thinking, Frederick leaped out of the cage and onto Millicent's shoulder. He sank his teeth into the soft, fleshy part of her upper arm.

She shrieked and dropped Ishbu. He landed on the floor and stood there, stunned. Frederick jumped off Millicent and landed beside his brother.

"He bit me!" Millicent Mallory screamed. Kay screamed too and ran over to console her. Jason Gumm (forgive him) laughed. Miss Dove dropped her yardstick and ran to the back of the classroom. The other children, seeing their chance, threw spit wads and paper airplanes and climbed on top of their desks.

Miss Dove handed Millicent a tissue and scooped the rats back into their cage before they got stepped on. "You'll need to see the nurse," she said. She gave Millicent Mallory a hall pass.

"I'll take her," said Kay Serah eagerly. Miss Dove agreed, and the girls left, Millicent still sobbing.

Miss Dove restored order in her classroom, and everything settled back to normal: the rats safe again in their cage, Ishbu snuggled up to Frederick, Frederick keeping watch with unblinking eyes; the children working on their geography definitions; Millicent Mallory and Kay Serah walking down to the nurse's office to get an ice pack.

But Frederick, who had meant to give Millicent a

simple warning nip—just enough to make her release Ishbu—had bitten Millicent harder than he realized.

OFF TO SEE
THE PRINCIPAL

EVERYONE KNOWS THAT ANIMALS who bite cannot be permitted in school. A biter would be unsafe. A biter could cause an infection. A biter might even carry rabies. So when the principal, Mr. Stern, stormed into Miss Dove's class, slamming the door behind him, Frederick hurried to the side of the cage.

"MISS DOVE!"

Miss Dove looked up from her desk, her brow creased and her cheeks flushed. The students froze, their eyes on Mr. Stern.

Frederick pressed his ear to the bars. Miss Dove in trouble? Because of him? He knew he'd violated the code of classroom pets—you must not EVER bite a child. But he and Ishbu were originally pet shop rats, bred to be held and cuddled, snuggled and loved. They didn't know how to deal with

19

someone like Millicent Mallory.

Mr. Stern was a tall man with gray hair, a gray mustache, gray eyes, and a gray suit and tie. Frederick thought he looked like the Rock of Gibraltar in the picture Miss Dove had shown them—craggy and forbidding. Now he slammed his palm down on Miss Dove's desk. She flinched.

"What is this I hear?" he demanded. "Harboring dangerous animals in my school? They must be eradicated! EXTERMINATED!"

"But, Mr. Stern!" said Miss Dove. "I'm sure it was an accident! Frederick and Ishbu have never bitten anyone before. Millicent must have done something to frighten them. She must have teased them or hurt them. I'm sure they'll never do it again."

Mr. Stern paid no attention. He grabbed the handle of the cage, swung the cage off the table, and carried it from the room. Frederick clung to the bars. His last sight of Miss Dove's classroom was the world map on the chalkboard.

The cage rocked like a boat as Mr. Stern marched down the hall, causing Ishbu's stomach to lurch. At the end of the hall, Mr. Stern opened a door with a glass pane. He went inside and set the cage on the desk with a bang. Ishbu jumped. Frederick's nose twitched. The room smelled like musty pencil shavings. The carpet was brown. The drapes over the one small window were brown.

The desk and chairs were brown.

Millicent Mallory sat on one of the brown chairs, swinging her legs. She had a small bandage on her arm. Kay sat next to her. Mr. Stern didn't even glance at them. He stood for a moment, rapping his fingers on top of the cage. Then he called out to his secretary in the next room: "Mrs. Lemon! Get the exterminators on the line. *Now.*" Finally he turned to the girls.

"Kay, go back to class."

"But I want to stay with Millicent," whined Kay. Mr. Stern didn't bother to answer. He just pointed at the door, and Kay walked out, giving Millicent a thumbs-up as she left.

"Oh, Mr. Stern!" called Mrs. Lemon from the next room. "Come quick! Elroy and Hubbard are brawling again!"

Mr. Stern looked at Millicent. "Wait here for your mother. She's on her way." He frowned at the rats. "I'll take care of you later," he said. He left, shutting the door behind him.

Frederick and Ishbu were alone in the principal's office.

With Millicent Mallory.

EXTERMINATED!

As soon as Mr. Stern closed the office door, Millicent ran over to the rat cage. She leaned close to the cage, so close that Frederick could smell the garlic on her breath from the pickle sandwiches she'd eaten for lunch.

"Ha, ha," she said. "You're gonna get it now, you filthy rats. Just wait until my mother comes. Bite *me*, will you?"

She picked up a ballpoint pen from Mr. Stern's desk and jabbed it through the bars of the cage. Ishbu jumped out of the way. Frederick hissed, showing his sharp white teeth. Millicent moved back a step. Then she scowled. "I'm not afraid of you, stupid old rats. You are going to be exterminated!"

"What does she mean?" whispered Ishbu. "What's *exterminated?*"

Ishbu always slept through Miss Dove's lessons,

including vocabulary.

"Exterminated, assassinated, eliminated, put down," Frederick whispered back. "Murdered." He trembled.

"They're going to KILL us?" Ishbu's eyes were enormous.

Frederick nodded. "It's all my fault," he said. "But we'll go down fighting. Fighting like rats."

Ishbu wiped his whiskers with his paw. "If it's all the same to you, Freddy, I'd rather not go down at all."

Millicent undid the latch on the wire door. They didn't know what she planned this time; she'd already been bitten once and wouldn't want to repeat the experience. Maybe she just hoped to scare Frederick and Ishbu. Maybe she wanted to poke them with the pen again.

Ishbu cowered at the far side. But Frederick stood his ground. His fur bristled, and he snarled, determined to protect himself and his brother. No matter what. Millicent shoved her hand into the opening, her fingers outstretched, reaching, closer and closer. . . .

Suddenly a door in the outer office banged. "Where's my baby?" cried a woman.

Millicent pulled her hand from the cage. "Mama!" She ran out of the principal's office.

The cage door swung open.

KAY'S BIG BROWN BOOTS

 NOW CAME THE MAD DASH through heater vents and tunnel-like pipes, the scramble through the open boiler room window, the moment when Frederick and Ishbu stood frozen, rooted to the playground asphalt by ancient instincts in the face of danger.

If only the shadow overhead had belonged to an eagle or a hawk swooping down upon them. A raptor might have been fooled into thinking the brothers were nothing more than oddly shaped sticks instead of two tasty rat morsels. (Probably not.)

Unfortunately it wasn't a bird of prey that sought to end their lives; it was Kay Serah.

Kay had been ordered back to class by Mr. Stern. And strictly speaking, she *was* on her way back to class. The long way back.

She had been reluctant to return without her best friend (whose mother, by the way, was now hurrying her out of the principal's office to the doctor and threatening to sue Miss Dove, Mr. Stern, and the whole school for harboring dangerous animals).

Kay hunched her bony shoulders and walked slowly across the playground in the drizzle, kicking a rock in front of her, hoping the recess bell would ring before she got back to class.

Why didn't Frederick and Ishbu run away as soon as they saw Kay?

Because even Frederick wasn't brave all the time. Alexander the Great wasn't brave *all* the time. Neither was Napoleon or Hercules. Even Superman isn't brave all the time. Frederick was frozen, just like Ishbu. Only the tips of his whiskers trembled.

Would Kay pass them by? She nearly did. Until the rock she was kicking rolled to a stop right in front of Ishbu.

Kay was not made of the same stuff as Millicent Mallory. She was a born follower. She laughed at all of Millicent's jokes, even though Millicent never made funny jokes. She carried and fetched for Millicent, and Millicent wanted a lot of things fetched. Everyone knows someone like that. There's even a name for them. Kay was Millicent's *toady*.

When Kay saw Frederick and Ishbu huddled

together, too frightened to breathe, she was afraid to pick them up. After all, she'd just seen Frederick bite Millicent—big, bossy Millicent, who wasn't afraid of anything or anybody. So she decided to stomp on the rats to be safe.

"I'll fix you," she muttered. "Bite my friend! We'll see about that!" Although she was a bully and a toady, Kay was also, in her own way, loyal.

"It's a good thing I wore my boots," she told the rats. "I bet I can crush you with one good stomp." And she raised her foot—

—just as the recess bell rang. Children poured through every doorway, a noisy, boisterous crowd. Distracted, Kay looked up and lost her chance. Frederick and Ishbu recovered their wits and dashed off. Kay raced after them, her brown boots clobbering the ground.

STOMP! STOMP! She missed again and again.

The terrified rats zigzagged across the playground. Ishbu didn't know whether he was coming or going. Frederick followed, trying to direct him into the bushes where they might find refuge.

Kay ran after them, yelling and stomping. The rats raced wildly across the asphalt. Who knows where it would have ended if it hadn't been for Jason Gumm.

The scrawny little boy with the runny nose was playing soccer with his friends in another part of the playground. Someone kicked the ball, and it bounced across the asphalt.

"I'll get it!" yelled Jason. He dashed after the ball, so intent that he didn't notice Kay running his way. And Kay was too busy chasing the rats to notice Jason, so naturally they collided. They hit so hard, Kay actually saw stars. Big red ones. She fell down and howled.

Jason rubbed his head and kept on running. The ball was in reach. He swung back his leg and kicked—

The soccer ball bounced once and caught Frederick in the stomach. Up he went into the air, and down, down, down he came, twisting and turning. Frederick saw the ground rapidly approaching. All he could do was hope he didn't break any bones or teeth or his tail. He closed his eyes. . . .

And that's why he missed the part where he didn't land.

THE SEWER

IT'S IMPORTANT TO NOTE THAT Wilberforce Harrison Elementary School was a really old school, crumbling and decaying. The playground was cracked, the chalkboards were dull, the linoleum floors were yellowed and peeling. The school also had an ancient sewer system.

All the water that went down the sinks and toilets flushed into big pipes underground, and from there into bigger pipes beneath the city streets. These huge culverts, like big underground streams, ran for miles until they eventually emptied into the river that fed the harbor at the edge of the city.

When it rained, the rainwater from the playground also flowed into the sewer, through grates embedded in the asphalt. Each grate had bars across the opening, like the portcullis of a castle, to keep large objects from falling in.

For example, the bars kept Jason Gumm and his soccer ball from falling into the sewer, while Frederick, tumbling from the sky after being knocked into the air, easily slipped between them. He slid right through, in a trickle of dirty rainwater, like a kid on a waterslide. He slipped down through the pipe and splashed into the greasy water.

He sank under the slime, but he refused to panic. He held his breath and opened his eyes. All he could see was water, as brown as chocolate milk. He bobbed up to the surface and gasped for air.

Rats can swim. At least Frederick could swim. He couldn't do the Australian crawl or the butterfly or even the frog kick. But he could dog paddle, sculling hard with his tiny arms and legs, using his tail like a rudder, his nose just above the surface. He swam around in a circle.

Where was Ishbu? Had he fallen into the sewer too? Frederick took a deep breath. "Ishbu!" he cried. The desperation in his voice echoed off the curved walls: "ISHBU! ISHBU! ISHBUUUUU!!!!"

There was no answer. Frederick was pulled along by the current beneath the city streets. Maybe Ishbu hadn't fallen through the grate. Maybe he was still on the playground at Wilberforce Harrison Elementary School, dazed and vulnerable, a sitting target for Kay's brown boots!

Or maybe he *had* fallen into the sewer, and—

being the weak, slightly overweight, and definitely out-of-shape rat that he was—maybe he had drowned. "Ishbu!" Frederick wailed again, but he could barely hear his own rat squeak over the noise of the gurgling water.

Suddenly the water sluiced through the pipe with the speed of a truck, as if a hundred toilets had flushed at once, or five thousand washing machines had finished the rinse cycle, or six thousand seven hundred bathers had pulled out the plugs in their tubs and let the water drain. Frederick spun in a whirlpool. Bubbles frothed around his head. He heard a sucking noise, and then he was rushed down the sewer, farther and farther from W. H. E. S. Farther from Miss Dove and her fifth-grade class.

Farther from Ishbu.

A STICK IN TIME

 Ishbu had watched in horror as Frederick flew up with the soccer ball, tumbled down, and slipped between the bars of the sewer grate.

"Don't leave me, Frederick!" he cried. He raced to the grate and peered in. He saw only the black hole of the sewer and heard only the evil chuckle of water, refuse, and sludge.

Kay recovered from her collision with Jason Gumm, and she heard Ishbu's squeak. "Dirty rat!" she yelled. "Now I've got you!"

As Ishbu saw her looming up behind him, he had but a second to choose: drain or doom? He put his paw over his nose and jumped—tail first—into the grate.

It was a tight fit, but he wriggled through just as Kay's big boot stomped. "Stupid rat," she growled. Cheated of her prey, she knelt down, grabbed a stick, and poked it through the grate. The stick touched nothing and, disappointed, she let it drop into the sewer.

Lucky for Ishbu she did. When he jumped into the water, he went right under, plunging nearly to the bottom, and came up again sputtering, choking, and coughing. He wasn't a swimmer like Frederick. He panicked and thrashed, getting water in his eyes and mouth and up his nose and generally making things worse.

Then the stick splashed into the water beside him. Ishbu grabbed it before it floated out of reach. He wrapped his forepaws and hind paws and even his tail around it and struggled to stay upright as he bobbled and spun in the current.

How he wished he were a fit and fearless rat like his brother!

"Freddy," he whispered, not daring to yell in case it threw off his balance. "Where are you? Come rescue me, please!" The constant gurgle of water was the only answer.

Gripping the thin stick, blinking and trembling, Ishbu floated rapidly downstream in the dark gloom of the sewer pipe. His one hope was that whatever came next couldn't possibly be worse.

DIRTY, ROTTEN SEWER RATS

THE RAT BROTHERS EXPERIENCED countless miseries on their separate journeys through the sewer pipe. Hours of cold, wet loneliness; cramped paws (Ishbu); a nearly frozen tail (Frederick); anxiety and fear (both). At least, being rats, the smell didn't bother them.

Frederick reached the end of the sewer line first. When he could hardly keep the tip of his nose above the murky water for another second, a dim, gray light appeared like a pale half-moon rising in the distance. The stream gathered speed. A roar filled his ears and, in a cascade of filth and water, he was ejected from the pipe into a slimy, bubbling pool.

He gasped with the shock of daylight, and immediately choked on the water. His legs were tired, so tired. It would be a relief to stop swimming. And if Ishbu *were* gone—why fight? For a moment

Frederick lost heart. He stopped paddling, closed his eyes, and sank beneath the surface of the scummy pond.

Ishbu had his stick, but his paws were blue with cold. And his frail craft spun in the current like a toy boat caught in a whirlpool, making him sick to his stomach.

"Oh, Freddy," he moaned. "Oh, Miss Dove! I wish I were back in my warm, dry cage!" Ishbu had conveniently forgotten the events that forced him to escape. If he had remembered Millicent Mallory and her toady, he might not have been quite so homesick.

At last the dark gloom gave way to a faint, pearly light and the round opening at the end of the pipe. As the water roared out, he lost his balance; and the stick tipped, striking him on the head. Dazed, he poured out of the pipe into the frothy pool below.

Ishbu splashed wildly, gasping. His cramped paws were useless. He sank down, down to the bottom of the sewage pond. His eyes closed, and bubbles burbled from his nose. He gave himself up for lost.

But then sharp teeth closed on the nape of his neck, and something, or someone, hauled him from the filthy pool and flung him onto the bank.

NEW DANGERS

THE RIVERBANK WAS A GRIM PLACE. Not lush or leafy, or the kind of place where one might spend a happy summer afternoon picnicking on the grass beneath a willow with a raft or canoe tied up for a jaunt later. No, the pool into which the rats had fallen was a backwater of the massive river that surged through the industrial area of the city. The bank was lined with factories belching soot and flame; black smokestacks; and huge, rusty metal wheels, pipes, and gears. Beneath brick factory walls, sewer pipes discharged evil-smelling filth into the settling pond. A few dead fish floated belly up on the surface of the scum.

The bank was littered with smashed cans, broken glass, discarded tires, washing machine parts, and the stuffing from abandoned sofas. A faded yellow sign announced: DANGER. NO TRESPASSING. But who would want to trespass here?

Ishbu lay on the dead grass. He blinked the water out of his eyes, coughed, and peered blearily up into a familiar whiskery face—

"Freddy!"

"Ishbu!"

The bedraggled rats embraced and rubbed whiskers. Frederick patted Ishbu's ears.

Ishbu clicked his teeth at Frederick in the friendly way rats greet each other. Tears filled his eyes. "You saved me!"

"Ah, it was nothing," said his brother. "I just jumped in and pulled you out." Embarrassed, Frederick began to comb his whiskers. Suddenly he stopped grooming and sat back on his haunches. "Ishbu, I was drowning too. I know I was. So who— or what—pulled *me* out?" The brothers stared at each other.

A low growl broke their silence.

Frederick scanned the bank. Clouds hung low and dark as if waiting to burst. The fading daylight revealed no new danger. The bank was deserted.

The growl came again, deep and menacing. The fur on Frederick's neck bristled. He peered into the sewer pipe. Within the dark hole two eyes glowed as red as coals.

Frederick backed up slowly until he was standing over Ishbu.

The red-eyed creature edged out of the pipe and stood on the bank. Fur as coarse as black wire covered it from head to rump. Its tail was as thick as a snake, with a stubby end where it had been cut or bitten off. Each enormous paw was tipped with razor-sharp claws. Frederick could tell from the scent that it was a rat—but what a rat! Twice the size of the brothers put together. Almost as big as a cat!

One blow from this creature's mighty paw and Frederick would be hawk food. One snap of his deadly teeth and Ishbu would be fish bait.

Frederick knew he might possibly outrun the giant rat, but Ishbu never could. They must fight then. It was obviously hopeless, but he had to try.

The huge rat advanced, red eyes gleaming.

"Halt!" cried Frederick. "Are you friend or foe?" (Frederick had been greatly influenced by Miss Dove's tales of Robin Hood and King Arthur.) He snarled in a way he hoped was threatening and raised his tail like a banner of courage.

The big rat paused. He opened his mouth. Pointed teeth glinted like knives in the dull light.

Then the rat did the last thing on Earth that Frederick expected.

THE BILGEWATER BRIGADE

 FREDERICK AND ISHBU WERE BORN in a pet shop—they had never been outside before. Miss Dove bought them when they were baby rats, so tiny that both of them could fit in the palm of her hand. Their fur was soft and silky, their eyes bright as buttons, their tiny ears as pink as wild rose petals. "Ooh, how sweet," Miss Dove had said, stroking each belly with a gentle finger.

They had gone straight from the pet store, a place full of familiar noises and smells, to the cage in Miss Dove's classroom. The only other animals that Frederick and Ishbu had ever seen were pet store animals such as hamsters, guinea pigs, parakeets, puppies, kittens, mice, and goldfish. Oh, yes—and Igor the boa constrictor. (More about him later.)

So although Frederick knew the black menace before him was a rat, he was completely unlike any creature the brothers had ever seen before.

From Miss Dove's lessons Frederick had heard about wharf rats, black rats, and Norway rats—large rats that frequented the harbors of cities and snuck onto vessels bound for faraway ports. But he'd never imagined a rat could be so huge and so terrifyingly ferocious.

"Do not come any closer!" Frederick called, his voice shaking only a bit. "Or we will be forced to defend ourselves!"

The wharf rat crossed his forepaws . . . and laughed.

He laughed and laughed. He laughed so hard he couldn't talk. He held his massive sides as if to hold in the laughter, but it was clearly all too much. He gave in and rolled on the ground, his feet punching the air.

"Ooh, mate, ain't you a beaut!" he said when he had caught his breath.

Frederick scowled and put up his paws. Like anyone who imagines himself a hero, he hated to be laughed at.

"Steady on, mate," said the wharf rat, scrambling back to his feet and wiping the tears from his eyes. "Keep making those fists at me, and you'll give yourself a cramp." He sniggered again. When he finally stopped, he added, "We could use a couple of ferocious blokes like you in the Bilgewater Brigade.

Ever think of joining up?"

Frederick shook his head. He wasn't ready to join anything. His pride was hurt. But Ishbu was more concerned with dinner than pride.

"Bilgewater Brigade? What's that? Will there be food?" Ishbu's stomach gurgled at the thought—crisp carrot sticks, sunflower seeds, maybe a chewy, stale marshmallow treat. (Miss Dove's students had always been generous with leftovers.)

The wharf rat winked. "Oh, sure, mate. Lots of food. Abso-bloody-lutely. Fish innards, sparrow eggs, smelly bits of bait nicely rotted by the sun—you want it, we got it. Anyhow, you're coming with me. I've got me orders. All newcomers must be approved by the Big Cheese himself."

The wharf rat smiled, showing his teeth. Frederick didn't smile, but Ishbu did.

"Now, mates, I can see you're harmless—maybe a few kangaroos loose in the paddock—but the Big Cheese will need to see for himself. Can't have any other gangs moving in on his turf, now, can he?" The wharf rat gestured to Ishbu to walk with him, and Ishbu, entranced by the prospect of a meal, fell into step.

But Frederick hung back. There was something wrong with this whole setup. Who was this Big Cheese? Was the wharf rat leading them into a rat-trap?

Ishbu was already halfway up the riverbank, happily chattering away with the big rat. Frederick saw no choice but to follow. The wharf rat was clearly his superior in size, strength, and ferocity. Frederick trotted after them, keeping an eye out for signs of treachery.

HEADQUARTERS

 FREDERICK SHIVERED AS THEY wound through the dank, narrow alley between the factories. Forbidding brick walls towered overhead. *Fortress walls*, thought Frederick. *Prison walls*. The sky was only a thin scrap above, gray in the early autumn dusk, leaving the alley in deep shadow.

A gust of wind whipped Frederick's fur. Yellowed newspapers scattered like dry leaves across his path. His stomach growled. He had to admit that he was hungry too. The brothers hadn't eaten since their escape from Miss Dove's classroom a lifetime ago.

An empty garbage can blew over and clattered down the alley. The three rats froze, their ears perked. A mangy striped cat stared at them from the top of a wooden crate. It sneered and hissed.

A cat! Frederick's heart pounded. He looked

around for someplace to hide, some way to escape.

But the gigantic wharf rat wasn't afraid. He faced the cat, his whiskers as taut as wire, his lips pulled back, showing his wicked yellow teeth. He snarled. Frederick had never heard that sound from a rat before. The cat slunk behind the crate.

"Don't worry about him, mate," said the wharf rat, nudging them on. "He knows better than to mess with a member of the Bilgewater Brigade."

Frederick and Ishbu stumbled forward, faster this time. Frederick kept looking back over his shoulder to make sure the cat wasn't stalking them. He still couldn't believe a rat could scare off a cat.

"Who is this Big Cheese you're taking us to?" asked Ishbu.

The wharf rat shot him a sidelong glance. "Ooh, mate. He's legend, he is. Runs this here territory. Has his fingers in all the pies."

Frederick shook his ears to show he didn't understand.

The wharf rat stopped. "He's the Big Cheese, get it?" Ishbu looked blank. The wharf rat sighed and sat down.

"The Big Cheese is the head of the Bilgewater Brigade. You haven't heard of us?" His voice rose to a squeak. "The most notorious gang in the city?"

Ishbu shrugged. "Sorry."

The wharf rat sniffed in disbelief. "Well, let me

enlighten you. The Bilgewater Brigade is made up of the most trusted hench-beasts of the Big Cheese. There's not a one of us who wouldn't die for him. He takes care of us, we takes care of him." He puffed out his chest. "I'm Lieutenant Nibs, at your service."

"But what does the Bilgewater Brigade do?" asked Ishbu.

"Do? Why we do it all," said Lieutenant Nibs. "Pestilence? That's us. Famine? Us again. Floods, disease, crop damage. All us." He nodded and pointed to himself. "Why, I personally oversaw the contamination of three cargoes of grain just last week." He slicked back his whiskers with his forepaws. "They don't call us vermin for nothing!"

"But that's awful!" Frederick said. Before now he'd had only a vague idea of the horrible crimes that some wild rats committed.

"Isn't it?" said Lieutenant Nibs proudly. He strode up and down the alley, eyes gleaming. "But really, plenty of rats could say the same. No, the genius of the Big Cheese is his criminal network. He's the Godfather, you might say. He rarely has to leave Headquarters, sitting there like a spider, spinning his webs."

"But why?" asked Ishbu.

The wharf rat sat down again and tucked his tail around his feet. He peered at Frederick and Ishbu with great seriousness.

"The Big Cheese hates humans. Has no use for them at all. Many's the time I've heard him say, 'The world would be better off without 'em.' Sometimes I thinks he'd exterminate all humans—if he could."

Frederick shuddered at the mention of this awful word.

Lieutenant Nibs gave a sly grin and jumped up. "We'd best get a move on, mates. Word will have gone ahead. He'll be expecting us." He led them farther down the twisting alley.

Frederick had to trot to keep up. He was silent, thinking about all that the wharf rat had told them. (Ishbu was silent too, thinking about how hungry he was and wondering if the Big Cheese would have some cheese for them.) Frederick remembered Miss Dove reading stories about Sherlock Holmes— his archenemy was Professor Moriarty, a criminal mastermind. *That's who the Big Cheese is*, he thought glumly. *What have we gotten ourselves into? And how will we ever get out?*

The rats came to a rusty, metal garbage bin pulled up against a chain-link fence. "In there," said Lieutenant Nibs. "Up you go." He gestured to a pile of empty cardboard boxes stacked like stairs against the side of the bin.

Ishbu, followed by Frederick, scrambled up the boxes to the rim of the bin. The rat brothers teetered there for a moment, and then the big wharf rat came up behind them and pushed them over the edge.

Frederick landed in a pile of soggy newspapers, coffee grounds, and slimy banana peels. Three large cockroaches scurried away. Ishbu shook himself all over and surreptitiously started nibbling a banana peel.

Frederick wondered if this was the trap. He quickly searched for a way out before Lieutenant Nibs slammed the lid on them. But to Frederick's surprise, the wharf rat jumped down into the rubbish beside them. "No time for that now, mate," he said, pulling Ishbu away from the peel. "Follow me."

He tunneled through the garbage to the bottom of the bin, where there was a hole in the metal—a large hole, like a doorway—big enough for a raccoon or cat (or even an opossum). Lieutenant Nibs led the way. Ishbu followed, a bit of banana peel stuck between his teeth. Frederick came after them, keeping the gray-pink tip of Ishbu's tail in view.

The hole led inside an old wooden building. The brothers and the wharf rat clambered over boards, loose bricks, metal pipes, and electrical wires. Dusty tracks, rat droppings, and a distinctive smell showed this was a well-traveled highway for rats—many rats. It was like the busy headquarters of a rat corporation. Except no one was in sight. This wasn't entirely strange, as it was still daylight outside (though just barely) and rats are nocturnal.

Lieutenant Nibs stopped at a closed door. "This is it," he said. He rapped on the door in a distinctive pattern—three knocks, a pause, three more.

It reminded Frederick of Miss Dove's demonstration of Morse code. He forgot where he was for a moment, overcome with the memory of Miss Dove—her gentle voice, her soft hands, her lessons in geography and literature.

Then the door opened.

THE BIG CHEESE

FREDERICK'S FIRST IMPRESSION came through his nose. (Rats have keen senses of smell and hearing, while their eyesight is relatively poor. In her classroom, Miss Dove always insisted that the children wash their hands before playing with the rats. Wash first, Miss Dove explained, so the rats would smell soap and not food. She knew that a rat scenting food might be tempted to nibble a tender finger.)

Frederick's senses were keener than most animals'. First he smelled food—the heavenly aroma of cantaloupe, strawberries, lavender, and warm chocolate chip cookies.

Next his sharp ears heard music—violins played softly from some distance away—Mozart, maybe, or was it Beethoven? Miss Dove often played recordings in her classroom.

Last of all he noticed the honey-colored light illuminating the room, highlighting the gold-and-red Persian carpet, the velvet chairs, the colorful tapestries hanging on the wall. Bookshelves filled with leather volumes lined the walls. This elegant room couldn't have looked less like a garbage dump.

"I can tell that you are a rat who appreciates the finer things in life," said a throaty voice from the shadows.

Frederick turned around. Sitting in an over-stuffed chair, holding a cane, was a large albino opossum the size of a small dog. His head wove back and forth like a snake, sniffing the air, listening. His eyes were milky white. Frederick realized that he was blind.

"You're the Big Cheese?" asked Ishbu. "I expected a rat."

The possum smiled, showing fifty sharp, yellow teeth. "Well, sir, I do have many rats in my organization—as well as ferrets, shrews, stoats, and weasels. Yes, even stray cats and wild dogs, abandoned by their owners. Our members have been poorly treated by humans, and we repay their kindness."

His smile chilled Frederick even more than his words.

"But first, gentlemen, let us have some refreshment!" said the possum. "You must be hungry after your adventures. And after you have eaten, I should like to hear of them." He rang a small bell on the table next to him.

Frederick wondered how the Big Cheese knew of their adventures; but before he could ask, a trio of shrews entered the room, pushing a tea cart loaded with food.

The shrews served Ishbu and Frederick sardine sandwiches, grapes dusted with sugar, iced lemonade, and banana bread. Ishbu ate until he was stuffed as full as a toy mouse. Frederick nibbled his food at first; but at last hunger overcame his suspicions, and he ate heartily too.

But even as he munched, he noticed that the Big Cheese took nothing more than a few sugared grapes and a cup of tea.

When the rat brothers were full to bursting, the Big Cheese poured them each a cup of tea from a china pot. "My special blend," he told them in his throaty purr. "Fine oolong from China, brewed with lemongrass and spices."

Frederick sipped. He'd never had tea before, never held a china cup. The handle was warm in his little paw. The elegant room, the soft music, the aromatic tea made him drowsy. He drifted as if on a cloud. The music continued softly, sweetly in the background.

"And now, gentlemen, tell me about yourselves,"

suggested the blind possum. "I'm always eager to meet new friends."

Ishbu chattered away happily about their school and their adventures. Frederick listened dreamily, his eyes half closed.

When Ishbu had finished, the possum was still smiling. "By gad, sir! What an amazing story," he said. "I'll tell you, I could use a couple of stout-hearted fellows like yourselves in my organization. Yes, indeed!" He took another sip of tea. "In fact, gentlemen, I have just the job for you. Just the sort of caper for two such brave and resourceful rats. It concerns an object of great value. . . ."

THE BURMESE BANDICOOT

"CENTURIES AGO," CONTINUED THE possum, "a maharajah in India fell in love with a beautiful woman. In her honor he commissioned a statue covered with gems: pigeon's blood rubies, Colombian emeralds, and diamonds of the first water. It took seventeen goldsmiths six years to create the statue in the shape of a legendary figure—the Burmese Bandicoot."

The possum leaned forward, his paws resting on his cane. "It is a rat made of solid gold, the rat known as a bandicoot in India. The statue is no bigger than a sparrow. It could be concealed in a bouquet of flowers or a sack of flour. Yet it is so valuable that kingdoms have been won and lost for it. By gad, sirs! If I told you half of what it is worth, you would not believe me!"

Drowsy no longer, Frederick sat forward in his

chair, holding his breath. He could almost see the small, jewel-encrusted figure gleaming and sparkling.

"Did she like it?" asked Ishbu. "Did the beautiful woman like it?"

The possum continued: "She did indeed, sir. But unfortunately, over the centuries the statue was lost.

"Until now. After years of searching, my sources have located the figure. All I need is someone to retrieve it. A simple matter—an ocean cruise, a quick recovery, a leisurely voyage home; and you, my dear fellows, would earn prestigious positions as trusted lieutenants in the Bilgewater Brigade!"

The possum's milky eyes were only inches from Frederick's. "You admire my room?" he whispered. "You enjoy my food, my music, my books? You too could live like this." He sat back and folded his forepaws over his well-padded stomach.

"But wouldn't it be stealing?" asked Ishbu. "Doesn't the statue belong to someone else now?"

The possum gave them a slow wink. "The current owners have no idea of its worth. It is wasted on them."

Frederick released his breath. The story stirred his imagination. His blood was racing. He was ready to sail, ready to steal—no, wait!—"recover" the statue. He scratched his ear, confused. He looked at

Ishbu. Ishbu shook his head ever so slightly.

"Well, gentlemen?" said the Big Cheese. "Does this interest you?"

There was a knock on the door. "Yes?" said the possum irritably. "What now?"

A black-faced ferret came in. Frederick and Ishbu knew it could gobble them up with a single bite, but the animal ignored them. "Sorry to disturb you, sir," he said. "There's trouble on level five. They need you."

"Do I have to do everything around here?" thundered the possum. He pushed himself up to his feet. "Oh, all right. Tell them I'm coming. And when I get there, heads will roll, sir! Heads will roll!"

He lumbered to the door. Just before he left, he turned his head toward Frederick and Ishbu, all trace of annoyance gone. "Gentlemen, help yourselves to another cup of tea. We'll discuss this further when I return." Then he waddled out the doorway, his cane tapping lightly, his heavy tail dragging across the floor behind him.

Frederick looked at Ishbu. Ishbu shook his head again, so strongly that his ears flapped. "No, Freddy, don't ask me."

"But Ishbu! An all-expenses-paid ocean cruise!"

"Freddy, listen to me. If it is so easy, why send us? Why not send his loyal hench-beasts? Why not send Lieutenant Nibs or the ferret?"

"You heard him, we're brave and resourceful. Stout-hearted fellows! Besides, we're smarter than all those other guys."

Ishbu nipped his brother gently on the shoulder. "He's lying, Freddy, and you fell for it. He wants us because it's dangerous. Too dangerous for his own animals. He wants to send us because we're expend . . . expend . . ."

"Expendable," said Frederick. "You mean he thinks it's okay if we get killed?" He scratched under his chin while he thought about this. "Why would he do that?"

"He's evil," whispered Ishbu. "You know I'm right."

Frederick crashed back to earth. He heard again the wharf rat's bragging as they walked through the alley: *Pestilence? That's us! Famine? Us again!*

They *were* evil.

Good old Ishbu! He wasn't fast or strong or even brave. But he had an unwavering sense of right and wrong as true as a compass.

"Of course," said Frederick. "I always knew it." But his voice was humble. "In my heart I did. It's just that I would like to travel. Someday . . ." His tone regained its usual confidence. "But *not* for the Big Cheese. We'll travel on our own. We want no part of the Bilgewater Brigade. We'll just have to tell him when he comes back." He shot Ishbu a sidelong glance. "But let me do the talking. We don't want to make him mad!"

The door opened, and the possum entered, scowling. But when he sat down in his chair, his expression changed, becoming mellow and gracious. He raised his nose and sniffed, weaving his head. Satisfied with whatever he sensed, he smiled in the direction of the rat brothers. There was a bit of blood on his teeth. He licked it off.

He just bit someone! thought Frederick. He hoped they weren't next.

"Well, gentlemen? Are you in?"

Frederick spoke carefully. "It's a very generous offer, I'm sure. We appreciate the honor. It's just that, well, we really must be going back to Wilberforce Harrison Elementary School. Miss Dove will be missing us."

For an instant Frederick saw a look of anger cross the Big Cheese's face. His eyes burned with a pale light, and he snarled softly. Then his mood altered as quickly as a cloud passing over the sun.

"How unfortunate," the Big Cheese said. "You would have been pillars of my organization." He rang the bell. "The ferret will show you out." His lips parted slightly, and he whispered: "I fear you are making a grave mistake."

Before Frederick could reply, the ferret opened the door and beckoned to the rat brothers.

They were dismissed. Frederick and Ishbu stood up, bowed slightly toward the unseeing possum, and followed the ferret out.

THE HOLE-IN-THE-WALL

ANXIOUSLY THE TWO RATS TRAILED the ferret down the hall. After all, ferrets were among their most feared enemies. Ishbu's heart raced, and Frederick swallowed hard. What if the ferret decided to eat them?

The ferret turned. His eyes were as round as twin moons. Frederick could see his own tiny reflection in each of them. Ishbu looked even smaller. The ferret's whiskers stuck out like broom straws. Frederick was nearly overcome by the creature's strong smell.

His instincts shouted: *Danger! Run! Hide!*

But the ferret only winked at them. "Never mind me," he said. "I have me orders. I've also had me dinner already."

It didn't reassure the brothers. They were well aware that a ferret didn't need to be hungry to kill rats. It would kill simply for sport. They were also aware that the Big Cheese had been more than a little put out when they turned down his proposal. It was obvious he didn't like being refused anything. Maybe he had ordered the ferret to kill them! So the brothers followed the ferret nervously, searching for possible escape routes and sheltering holes.

Now that it was night the hallway was no longer deserted. It bustled with the sound of feet pattering to undercover places and small bodies slinking through the shadows.

The smell of animal activity was strong as well. Frederick scented rats, mice, shrews, and larger animals such as stoats, weasels, and cats. He sneezed. Maybe even a dog! *The Bilgewater Brigade.* What crimes had the Big Cheese ordered up for tonight?

The ferret led them out a different exit from the garbage bin where they'd entered—a narrow gap between two boards. Once outside Frederick sniffed the night air. A wisp of fog curled up the alley, bringing with it the scent of the harbor. A distant foghorn boomed—a cold, lonely sound.

"Off you go," said the ferret. "Say, if you fellas need a bunk for the night, try the Hole-in-the-Wall Inn. It ain't fancy, but the food is good and the company even better. Tell 'em Felix sent you." He gave them directions, winked again, and slipped back inside.

Frederick and Ishbu scurried down the alley, keeping close to the buildings so they wouldn't attract attention. Following the ferret's directions, they soon found the inn.

It *was* a hole in the wall—only slightly larger than a mouse hole. The inviting, warm glow of firelight streamed into the dark night. The enticing aroma of fried fish followed. Frederick and Ishbu ducked inside.

They stood in the entrance. The walls were half-timber and whitewashed with rough beams overhead. Bright copper pans hung over the hearth where a merry fire burned. In the center of the room stood several large wooden tables, all filled with noisy creatures. There were snatches of song, and the smells of wood smoke, fish-and-chips, and ale.

Frederick led the way, winding between the animals here and there. Ishbu bumped into a table, and a mug of ale slopped over, spilling foam.

"Hey! Watch it, buster!" shouted a brown rat with a patch over one eye. The burly rat stood up and shook his fist.

"Sorry, sorry," said Ishbu.

The brown rat narrowed his good eye and sat back down. "Oh, a pet store rat!" He spat. "Cat bait! He's too little to bother with!" His friends all laughed.

Ishbu wiped his forehead and crept after Frederick.

They sat together at an empty table and looked around. All sorts of animals were drinking, eating, laughing, arguing, or singing sea chanteys. Frederick saw big, rough-looking ferrets and weasels and tiny, fierce predators such as voles and shrews. A couple of the rats looked like the seafaring type, with gold earrings and vicious scars. One rat even had a peg leg! Not the sort of creatures you'd want to meet on a dark night in a dark alley.

The bar-mouse came over and took their order. "Two root beers," said Frederick. "And do you have a room for the night?"

"I'll see if we do," she said briskly. She had clearly once been a white rat, although now her coat was soiled and dull. Her eyes, however, were still bright and shiny pink. She brought back the root beers, foaming over the top, and set them before the two thirsty brothers. "No rooms left," she said.

Ishbu looked ready to cry. "Freddy, I'm so tired. I don't think I can go any farther."

Frederick stared up at the bar-mouse. She stood, one paw on her hip, smacking a wad of bubblegum. "Felix sent us," he told her.

The bar-mouse's pink eyes opened wide, and she grinned. Some of her teeth were missing. "Well, why din'cha say so? Of course you can 'ave a room! Any friend a Felix is a friend a ours!" She went off to book the room.

Frederick turned to Ishbu. "What now?" he said.

Ishbu slurped his root beer. When he set down his mug, foam dripped off his whiskers.

"You have a root beer mustache," Frederick said, giggling.

Ishbu grinned and crossed his eyes.

The brothers had been through a lot that day—they'd been tormented, hungry, wet, and nearly scared to death. They'd even talked to a ferret! At that moment a root beer mustache seemed like the funniest thing in the world.

They laughed and laughed. They roared until their sides hurt. They snorted, chuckled, hooted, and guffawed. "No, no, no more," hiccupped Frederick. Ishbu crossed his eyes again, and Frederick lost it. They giggled some more, unaware of the glances from the other animals.

Ishbu got root beer up his nose. Suddenly he started to cry.

Frederick stroked his fur. "It's okay, Ishbu. It's okay." Ishbu wiped his eyes with the tip of his tail.

"We'll stay here today and rest up," said Frederick. "Tonight we can ship out on one of these cargo ships. We're free, Ishbu! We can finally see the world!"

Ishbu's dark eyes swam with tears. "An ocean voyage? I'd get seasick, I know it. Let's go home, Freddy. We don't belong here. We aren't wild rats.

We belong in a nice, warm, safe cage in Miss Dove's classroom. No cats, no shrews, no ferrets, and no Mr. Big Cheese!"

Ishbu started grooming himself. Whenever Ishbu was upset, he groomed. First he licked his forepaws, then—stroke, stroke—he sleeked down his ears and whiskers.

"But we can't go back," Frederick said softly. He nuzzled Ishbu under his ears. "Mr. Stern wants us exterminated. And what about Millicent Mallory and Kay Serah?"

Ishbu stopped grooming. His whiskers fluttered. "They don't seem too bad compared to the Bilgewater Brigade!"

But images of sea cruises, palm trees, soft winds, and southern constellations still danced in Frederick's head. The romance of new places, new scents to sniff, new sounds to hear, new things to see! How could he return to Miss Dove and her lectures knowing he had missed out on a real adventure?

He couldn't give in and go back. Not yet. This might be his only chance. Ishbu was just tired out, that was all. Give him a good day's sleep and he'd see it differently. Frederick nipped Ishbu playfully on the ear. "Come on, brother rat, scaredy-cat. Let's turn in."

The bar-mouse showed them to their room. Through the tiny, dirty window the gray light of dawn appeared. The nest of filthy, torn-up papers in the corner looked thin and shabby. Ishbu sniffed it. A big black cockroach scurried out. The room wasn't clean or nice or homelike.

Frederick felt a pang as he thought of the bedding in their cage composed of old newspapers, falling-apart textbooks, atlases, and dictionaries, constantly renewed to provide a fresh bed, and—incidentally—an ever-changing source of reading material. He sighed. Maybe they should go back.

But what about his dream to see the world? And what about Millicent Mallory? He shook his head. He was exhausted too. Things would become clearer after a good day's sleep.

Ishbu fell asleep as soon as he hit the paper. Frederick had one last thought before he drifted off—*at least we are done with the Big Cheese.*

RATNAPPED!

 WHEN FREDERICK WOKE UP, VIVID pink and orange streaks of sunset shone through the dirty window pane. He had slept all day. His head ached. He scratched behind his ears and then stretched, opening his mouth in a huge yawn. He peered around.

He was alone in the room.

Ishbu was gone!

A note fluttered to the floor from the windowsill. Frederick snatched it up and read:

My dear Mr. Frederick,
I do hope this note finds you in good health. Do not be alarmed by your brother's disappearance. He is in good paws and will be well cared for. If you want to see him

again, you know what to do.
As always,
The Big Cheese

P.S. Mr. Ishbu sends his regards and begs
you to be quick about the matter.

Frederick crumpled the note in his paw and gnashed his teeth. Those villains! Ishbu had been ratnapped!

co

As to how the dastardly deed was done:
When Mary, the bar-mouse, heard Felix's name the night before, she knew exactly what to do. Because the ferret wasn't really named Felix. He was Edgar. "Felix" was a code word from the Bilgewater Brigade. It meant they wanted Mary to slip someone a mickey. The knockout drops would make the drinker sleep for hours. Meanwhile, the bad guys could pick his pocket, lift his wallet, or even shanghai the sleeping animal.

co

Frederick paused in his pacing and peered out of the tiny window. He could just make out the busy harbor glowing in the orange sunset. Cargo ships lined the docks, and cranes and derricks stood silhouetted against the sky like bare winter trees. A seagull cried out. The call sounded like weeping.

Once these sights and sounds would have stirred Frederick's heart. To see the great ships that sailed around the globe! To be so close to his dream—world travel!

But now his heart lay leaden in his chest. What was the use of adventure without Ishbu?

But Ishbu doesn't want to travel, whispered a small, nagging voice in Frederick's head. *Ishbu wants to be safe, warm, dry, and well fed.* And wasn't that what the Big Cheese promised?

Frederick read the note again.

The nagging voice went on: *Seek the Burmese Bandicoot alone! Ishbu will be "well taken care of," and you—Frederick the Brave—can take the sea voyage you've always wanted. Find the statue, bring it back, and rescue Ishbu. You'll be a hero! And you'll get to see the world. What could be better?*

Nervously he nibbled his toenails. Frederick, although strong and smart and brave, was never good at tough decisions. If only Ishbu were here to help him! But if Ishbu were here, he wouldn't need rescuing, would he? Oh, it was all too confusing.

∞

In fact, Ishbu was not safe, warm, dry, or well fed at all.

He was at that very instant imprisoned in the top story of one of the abandoned warehouses that lined the waterfront. Frederick could have seen the building from his window—if he'd known where to look.

Ishbu was tied in a grain sack, heaped on a stack of sacks that looked exactly like the one he was in. He was gagged and bound paw and foot. His nose itched from the grain dust inside the sack, and his stomach growled from hunger. Also, his paws hurt where the rope cut into them. His ratnappers had been rough—they'd rat-handled him, so to speak—and he was bruised all over. No bones were broken, but he could feel a trickle of blood from a cut on his head.

He struggled, but he was bound too tightly to free himself. The gag prevented him from gnawing, and also from squeaking. So he did the one thing he could think of. He cried. Big tears dripped down his nose. He couldn't help himself. He wasn't like Frederick. He was lonesome and scared. He cried until the bandanna binding his muzzle was soggy.

∽

Frederick's thoughts circled around and around like a swarm of bees. Which task should he attempt first: rescue Ishbu or seek the Burmese Bandicoot? That was the question.

Enough! He was wasting time. He had to find Ishbu, even if it meant losing the chance for an ocean voyage. So be it! Happy to have made a choice at last, he smoothed the note and read it once more.

The note offered no clues to Ishbu's where-abouts. Frederick gave a final glance out of the rapidly darkening window to the ships in the harbor. Then he did what a rat does best: he sniffed. Nose to the ground, he headed out into the night.

A KEEN NOSE

FREDERICK'S KEEN NOSE HAD NO problem picking up Ishbu's trail and following the strong smell outside. He wound through the alley like a bloodhound on the scent of an escaped convict. At one point he thought he'd lost the trail. Then he realized that someone had tried to disguise Ishbu's odor with lavender oil. They hadn't counted on an expert tracker such as Frederick! He sneezed twice (lavender is strong) and then recognized this as a fragrance he'd encountered before, in the headquarters of the Big Cheese. He snuffled again and caught a whiff of Ishbu. He hurried on.

The trail led downhill, through narrow passageways and between forbidding buildings. It was completely dark now. The fog had blown off, and the moon had not yet risen. Frederick heard many creatures afoot—on dark expeditions of their own—but he saw nothing except shadows.

He followed Ishbu's trail down to the waterfront, where it disappeared beneath the odors of smelly fish, rotting food, and the stench of fresh skunk. The Ishbu-scent was all muddied up with these new smells. Frederick lost all trace of lavender oil.

He stopped at a row of warehouses. They leaned together in the dark like a group of gossiping neighbors, but their broken windows were like vacant, empty eyes. Frederick huddled on a curbstone. He scrubbed his nose with his paws and sniffed again, trying to sort out the complicated odors.

Fish. Seagulls. The ocean. Sand. Animals: ferrets, cats, dogs, mice, wharf rats, weasels, stoats, the musk of skunk—but not a trace of Ishbu.

And yet some sixth sense told him Ishbu was here.

Somewhere.

TRAPPED LIKE A RAT

IT MUST HAVE BEEN CATS THAT gagged Ishbu. A rodent would never have made such a mistake. For the ratnappers had stuffed his mouth using a *cotton* bandanna. As any rodent knows, cotton is easy to gnaw through; and what's more, it tastes good.

When his gag became soggy with tears, it was relatively easy for Ishbu to gnaw through it. Actually, he chewed it right up and swallowed it. It didn't taste as good as a leftover bologna sandwich or a slightly mashed banana from a fifth-grader's lunch, but it was better than nothing.

After that it didn't take him long to nibble through the cords binding his paws and feet. They were rubber-coated wire cords, which might have stopped a cat or dog but posed no problem for a rat. Ishbu even munched the rubber coating for extra energy.

Next he chewed a hole through the grain sack. Now he was free! He shook all over, removing the grain dust from his coat. Then he sat back and groomed, rubbing his paws over his nose and whiskers and ears.

He wasn't just being vain or giving in to nerves. He needed his ears and nose as clean as possible for sensing danger. And his whiskers—delicate feelers extending his sense of touch—needed to be free of dust and dirt.

He stood on top of the sacks and sniffed. He was alone in the empty storehouse room.

The only light came through a dirty glass skylight. Ishbu balanced on the tiptoes of his hind paws and stretched. He could see a broken pane, just big enough for a rat to crawl through. If only he could . . . He jumped like a kangaroo rat, again and again—leaping, straining, arching. But it was no use. The skylight remained tantalizingly out of reach. Moonlight drifted through the dust, filtering down from the ceiling in lovely golden shafts.

Ishbu ignored the moonlight. He wasn't interested in romance or poetry. He was interested in escape. Those animals who had bound and locked him in a warehouse were clearly up to no good. He couldn't be there when they came back to finish the job, whatever it was!

He scrambled down the sacks and hunted around the walls of the room. Not a hole, not a crevice, not a gap. Oh, there was a door, but it was shut; and the doorknob was too high for a rat to reach. And Ishbu knew without even trying that the door would be locked.

He took an experimental bite of the bottom of the door. If he had enough time, a week or a month—maybe two—he might be able to gnaw a hole big enough.

But the bottom of the door was bound with metal to keep the rats from the grain.

There was no way out. No escape.

Ishbu sat back on his haunches and howled.

He was trapped.

THE HOWL OF THE RAT

MOST HUMANS HAVE NEVER heard a rat howl. It is both high-pitched and quiet. On a scale of one to ten—with a ten being the anguished howl of a wolf whose mate is shot by hunters and a one being the thin whisper of an ant seared by the rays of a magnifying glass—Ishbu's howl was only a two.

It couldn't compete with the noises of the wharf: the grunts and groans of ships straining at their ropes; the whir of giant cranes loading cargo; the grind of gears on forklifts and tractors; the thumps and bangs as crates and sacks and boxes hit the deck.

But down on the moonlit street in front of the empty warehouses Frederick heard.

And he knew who it was. "I'm coming, Ishbu!" he cried, springing to his feet. He scaled the wall of the first warehouse. The wood was rough and old, offering plenty of pawholds. He scrambled up until he reached the roof.

He scampered along the rooftops, sniffing and listening for Ishbu's howl. He sprinted around smokestacks and chimneys, and crept past broken tiles and holes in the shingles.

He heard the tattoo of tramping paws—a patrol of wharf rats! He saw them just in time and dodged behind a chimney pot. The rats marched by like soldiers in formation, their paws beating a cadence on the roof. Frederick recognized Lieutenant Nibs and saw him sniff the air suspiciously, his whiskers twitching; but the patrol didn't stop.

When they were gone, Frederick crept out from behind the chimney. He hoped Ishbu wouldn't howl again. Suppose the wharf rats heard him!

He trotted along silently, skittering over the shingles, peeking into every skylight. "Ishbu?" he whispered. The skylights revealed nothing but dusty, dirty panes of glass draped with cobwebs as filmy as old lace curtains. It was hopeless. Ishbu was here. But how would Frederick ever find him?

The moonlight made a checkerboard of light and shadow on the roof, exaggerating shapes and lines. Frederick ran through it—black, white, black, white. He jumped the gap to the roof of the last warehouse.

The skylight had a broken pane of glass.

Frederick put his long nose inside and crinkled it, sniffing. Grain dust, wheat, and maybe a little rye. The slightly moldy smell of rotting wood. Saltwater, ancient rat droppings, and—yes!—lavender oil!

"Ishbu!" he hissed. "Are you there?"

Ishbu's voice echoed like a rusty hinge: "Oh, Freddy! I'm here! I'm here!"

Frederick, peering inside, could just make out Ishbu scrambling up a stack of grain sacks. "Up here!" Frederick called. "Let's get you out of this. Give me your paw!"

Ishbu reached for the skylight, and Frederick leaned down, careful not to cut himself on the broken glass. He stretched his foreleg into the room as far as he could. It was no good. Their paws were still much too far apart.

"Jump!" he called. Ishbu jumped, and the tips of their claws brushed lightly; but then Ishbu tumbled back down on the grain sacks, too fast for Frederick to catch him.

Frederick heard the beat of marching paws again. The troop of wharf rats! They were coming back!

"Quick, Ishbu!" he yelled. "Grab my tail!" Frederick turned around and dangled his tail into the room.

Ishbu jumped, missed, and jumped again. This time he caught the end of Frederick's tail. He scrambled up. Ignoring the pain, Frederick clawed his way up the roof, pulling Ishbu behind him like a fish on a line.

Rat-a-tat! Rat-a-tat! The thrum of paws grew louder, and the wharf rats came around the chimney.

"Lieutenant! I see them!" shouted a rat. "Over there!"

"Get them!" ordered Lieutenant Nibs. And the chase was on.

Ishbu and Frederick raced across the warehouse roof in the moonlight. They shinnied down a drainpipe as fast as their paws could go. Ishbu fell into the rain barrel and Frederick pulled him out, wet as a drowned rat. The wharf rats were right behind them, eyes gleaming, teeth glinting.

"Through here," panted Frederick. He led Ishbu down an alley to the dock. The wharf rats must have sounded an alarm, because Frederick could hear other animals joining the chase—ferrets and cats, stronger, bigger, faster creatures. They were doomed! His heart hammered like a pile driver, and his breath stabbed his side. His paws ached. He knew Ishbu must be even worse off.

The smell of the ocean was sharp in Frederick's nose, and he heard the slap of waves against the dock. The two rats raced through the narrow, twisting alley to the dockyards. Cobblestones gave way to weathered wood. Behind them came the pounding of many paws.

Frederick tripped over a coil of rope and caught himself. The rope stretched across a few feet of open water to a ship tied to the dock.

"This way!" he called to Ishbu. Perhaps they could escape by boarding the ship. He and Ishbu could climb ropes, but cats and ferrets couldn't. The army of wharf rats was another matter; the rodents could climb anything that the brothers could. But it was their best chance.

Frederick scrambled up the rope, gripping it with all four paws, hanging upside down like a spider on a web above the dark, cold water.

"Freddy!" called Ishbu.

Frederick inched across the rope and swung himself aboard the ship. He sat back on his haunches, breathing hard. He could just make out Ishbu standing on the dock. The ship's horn blasted as Lieutenant Nibs, followed by his army of wharf rats, burst out of the alley and raced toward Ishbu.

"Come on, Ishbu!" called Frederick.

"No, Freddy!" cried Ishbu. "You know I can't do it!"

A sailor on board the ship untied the rope and tossed the end to a dockhand. The rope lay limp and useless on the dock, no longer a lifeline over the water.

Frederick ran to the ship's rail. "You'll have to jump for it, Ishbu," he cried. "The ship is sailing! Jump, now!"

Ishbu looked over his shoulder. The wharf rats were nearly upon him. He gathered whatever strength he had left and raced toward the edge of the dock. Squeezing his eyes closed, he leaped for the ship.

Ishbu flew across the widening channel of water. Frederick stretched out his forelegs as if he could pull his brother to him, and it appeared to work. The next second Ishbu crashed into the ship's railing, caught it, and clung fast, wrapping his tail around the rail. Frederick hauled him aboard by the scruff of his neck, and they collapsed together on the deck of the ship.

The horn blasted again, and the ship steamed away from the dock.

Frederick and Ishbu untangled themselves, panting.

"I can't believe you jumped across," said Frederick. "I've never seen you do anything like that."

Ishbu's ears turned pink in the warmth of Frederick's praise.

"We must hide," warned Frederick.

Ishbu pulled him to the side of the ship. "But look, Freddy! We don't have to worry anymore. We made it! We're safe!"

Frederick looked over at the dock. The Bilgewater Brigade—wharf rats, cats, ferrets—had not tried to follow them aboard. Quite the opposite. They sat on the dock, laughing and waving, as if seeing friends off on a cruise. Even Lieutenant Nibs was grinning.

What was going on? Where was this ship going? Why were they so *happy* that the brothers had escaped?

Unless they hadn't escaped at all.

Part Two: SEA

To be a sailor of the world,
bound for all ports . . .
                    —Walt Whitman

SMALL STOWAWAYS

MOONLIGHT SPARKLED ON THE billowing waves. The lights of the great city disappeared behind them. The wind ruffled Frederick's fur, salt spray tickled his nose, and the plaintive cry of gulls pierced his ears. A sea voyage! His spirits soared.

Ishbu was another matter. He was seasick before the ship left the harbor.

"Poor Ishbu," murmured Frederick. Clouds blew across the moon, and it began to drizzle, not enough to drench the rats but a soft, misting rain that made them shiver.

"Let's get under cover. We'll find someplace safe, and maybe something to eat," said Frederick. After all, they were stowaways and could not expect a warm welcome. Frederick looked around the ship's deck and spotted a likely looking hole.

The ship chugged beneath the big orange bridge and set out into the rough seas of the open ocean. No more smooth sailing. The ship lunged up the crest of each wave, plunged down into the trough, and rose again. The sailors were used to it; but to a couple of landlubbers such as Frederick and Ishbu, it was as wild as a storm. The motion churned Ishbu's stomach like a washing machine. Frederick led him across the deck toward the hole, keeping an eye out for humans.

The hole was no bigger than a cucumber, but rats can fit into spaces nearly as small as the burrow of an earthworm. It was also damp, dark, and cramped. It smelled of rust and old fish, and something else—pipe tobacco? Ishbu didn't care. For once he wasn't hungry. He curled up, his tail over his nose to keep it warm, and fell asleep.

Frederick anxiously chewed his toenails. *The Bilgewater Brigade gave up too easily. What do they know that we don't?* he wondered.

It was too much to think about now. He'd talk it over with Ishbu in the morning.

Frederick settled down next to Ishbu. Soothed by the rhythm of his brother's snores, he too was soon fast asleep.

He didn't see the paw slipping stealthily into their sanctuary—a six-toed paw, each toe tipped with a claw as curved and sharp as a scimitar.

Silently it reached—exploring, poking, searching, searching. . . . Silently it withdrew.

Frederick and Ishbu slumbered on.

SEA CRUISE

ALTHOUGH RATS ARE NOCTURNAL by nature, they will adapt to their situation. In the classroom Frederick and Ishbu usually slept at night and stayed awake during the day to listen to Miss Dove. Well, Frederick did anyway. (Ishbu only stayed awake in case anyone decided to feed him.)

Now the exhausted rats slept all night. Unaccustomed to the ship's motion, Frederick woke early the next morning. He peered out and saw a sky as dull and gray as a pigeon's wing and a leaden sea to match. He woke Ishbu with a nip on his flank.

"Is it breakfast, Freddy?" Ishbu rubbed the sleep out of his eyes.

"Let's go see what we can find," said Frederick. "There's a crew, so there must be food. Let's find the galley."

Frederick remembered Miss Dove's vocabulary

lessons: *galley* meant kitchen; *bulwarks* were the low, metal walls to keep people (and rats) from being washed overboard; *scuppers* were the holes in the bulwarks to let the water run off. *Port* was left and *starboard* was right. *Bow* meant the front of the ship and *stern* meant the back.

"We'll find the galley below," he told Ishbu. *Below* was downstairs inside the ship. "Watch your footing; we don't have our sea legs yet."

The rat brothers tumbled out of their hole. A steady breeze made them shiver. Frederick blinked the saltwater spray from his eyes. The only humans were a couple of sailors swabbing the other end of the deck. The coast was clear.

"Look for a hatch," Frederick whispered. He led the way, creeping around masts and over coiled ropes.

The brothers found the hatch, slipped through, and raced down the stairs to the galley. They were in luck! The galley was empty. Cautiously they ran across the floor. Ishbu was pleased to spot a garbage can overflowing with tasty scraps.

While Ishbu feasted, Frederick looked around.

Frederick realized that they must have come aboard an old cargo ship. It was rusty, out-of-date, and dirty. A perfect place for rats, it seemed. Frederick's whiskers twitched with excitement as he wondered where they were bound.

(In fact, the *General Custer* was a tramp steamer, a ship that stayed off the main shipping routes and sailed from port to port, picking up cargoes here and there and delivering them to distant lands. What Frederick didn't know was this: some tramp steamers are used in illegal dealings such as piracy and smuggling.)

The day passed, and the next. The ship took them farther and farther away from Miss Dove's classroom and the easy life they knew.

Ishbu was too sick to care. After his first meal he spent his time napping in their little hole and nibbling the light but sustaining tidbits Frederick fetched for him from the galley.

When he wasn't foraging for food or hiding from the ship's crew, Frederick clung to the ship's rail, his ears flapping in the breeze and his eyes on the misty horizon or the glassy swell of water streaming past the prow. He spent hours watching seabirds wheel overhead, letting the sun warm his fur. He was having an adventure!

Or was he? Worry still gnawed at him. Where were they going? And what would happen to them when they got there?

On the fifth day out of port, Frederick and Ishbu crept across the deck, headed for the galley. Ishbu's tummy had settled down, and they planned to browse the garbage can buffet. Without warning they heard the heavy thump of footsteps coming toward them and smelled the pungent odor of tobacco. A sailor!

The brothers had been lucky. The *General Custer* didn't have rat guards on the tending lines—those cone-shaped pieces of metal preventing rats from climbing aboard. But Frederick was certain that the sailors used traps on board, and maybe even poison!

The steps came closer. If the sailor saw them, they were dead meat. Frederick spotted an opening in the bulwark. It yawned like a port in a storm. A hiding place?

"Hurry, Ishbu," whispered Frederick.

But they were too late. The bright sunlight—so warm on their fur, so harsh to their eyes—illuminated the rats like a spotlight. If only they'd stayed in their hideaway until night as they were supposed to! But they had seen so few humans on the voyage so far that they'd gotten careless.

"Rats!" roared the sailor. "Blast and keelhaul! I'll not have filthy vermin on *this* vessel!" A shoe—hard and heavy—whistled past Frederick's head.

"Run!" squeaked Ishbu, as if his brother needed the warning. They both raced across the open deck.

The hole loomed, promising safety, but the steps pounded right behind them. They could feel the sailor's feet shaking the deck.

"Jump!" yelled Frederick.

PANIC

It wasn't a hole at all. It was the opening of a narrow pipe that ran steeply through the walls of the ship like a tube slide at an amusement park. The rats zipped down, twisting and turning, tails first, one after the other. It was dark and a bit cold, but they slid down so quickly that they barely had time to notice.

"Watch out!" yelled Frederick as Ishbu's toes jammed in his ear.

"Sorry, Freddy! I can't stop!" cried Ishbu as his tail snapped Frederick's nose. Abruptly the pipe ended, and the rats crashed to the floor.

Frederick crouched, getting his bearing. They were on the floor of a narrow, dank room. The pipe ended a foot or so above them.

Only a whisper of light penetrated the gloom. Even though he couldn't see much, Frederick's senses told him the room was tiny, hardly bigger than a closet. A storage room? His nose twitched. He could smell grease and metal. And something else.

A cat!

There was no mistaking that horrible odor. He could hear its breath, rasping like a saw, somewhere in the darkness.

Ishbu edged next to Frederick, his body quivering like a hummingbird's wings. An itchy, stuffy smell filled his nose—and Ishbu sneezed.

The cat pounced, missing the brothers by a whisker's breadth.

The rats panicked. They couldn't freeze, so they'd have to—

"RUN!" shouted Frederick. The rat brothers raced around the room, pursued by the cat. In their frenzy they couldn't find any place to hide. The pipe they'd fallen from was far above their reach.

Circling the room made them dizzy, and the overpowering stench of cat made them crazy. Frederick's mind went blank. Instinct took over: RUN! RUN! RUN!

Ishbu's fur stuck up wildly. He whimpered in fear. Frederick hissed, but the cat stayed on their tail, racing, racing.

They lost all sense of direction, their breath tearing from their lungs in shallow, ragged gulps as they darted back and forth across the floor. No holes, no cracks, no crevices, no gaps. And everywhere the horrid, overwhelming stink of cat.

SMACK! A huge, furry paw hit the floor. The rats skidded to a stop, turned, and dashed to the left. *SMACK!* The cat's other paw slammed the floor. They turned back. A huge and furry body blocked their way. Frederick threw himself in front of Ishbu to protect him. *SMACK!* A heavy paw slammed down on them, pinning them to the floor.

They had run straight into the paws of death.

No escape, no exit—even if they'd had the energy.

And they didn't. Frederick could barely breathe, he was so worn out; and he could feel Ishbu panting and sweating behind him.

Was this the end? Were they to meet their deaths as cat food?

Frederick gave a brief sigh for his lost dreams— the sea cruise, the world tour, adventure! Freedom! So close and yet so far!

Ishbu would have given a similar sigh for the lost luxuries of Miss Dove's classroom—the marshmallow treats, the carrot sticks, the leftover ice-cream cups—but he was too frightened to think of anything at all. He squeezed his eyes shut and waited for the final, fatal blow or the cruel crunch of teeth around his tender neck.

But the cat stayed motionless, its heavy paws nearly crushing the brothers. Frederick carefully opened his eyes. Better to face death bravely, like a rat, not a mouse!

In the gloom he could just make out the huge cat face above him, the whiskers stiff as needles, the teeth like bowie knives. A shudder ran through Frederick from nose to tail. Still he forced himself to keep looking, staring into the single eye that gleamed as blue as an evil flame.

THE NIGHTMARE KING

Miss Dove always said, history matters. And in this case it is necessary to go back a bit in Frederick and Ishbu's story and meet Igor, the boa constrictor who had been with them in the pet shop.

Igor was enormous, with a brown-and-green pattern on his scales like a crocodile's. He had lived in the pet shop for many years, and no one had ever tried to buy him. Year after year people bought the other snakes—corn snakes and king snakes, ball pythons and milk snakes—but no one made an offer for Igor. Customers took one look at his narrow, darting tongue, his curved teeth, and his flat, obsidian eyes and turned away.

Igor lived in the largest tank. The pet shop owner kept feeding him and feeding him—first mice, then rats, and finally whole rabbits. He had grown to nearly twenty feet long—longer than most boa constrictors. Igor grew bigger and meaner every year. Also craftier, crueler, *and* crazier.

Igor considered himself the emperor of the pet shop.

One sunny September morning, in a cage two shelves away from Igor, Frederick and Ishbu were born—the only males in a litter of fifteen pups. Mama rat was white with pink eyes and a long, bare tail. Her pups were hairless, and their eyes were closed. She would fall asleep while the pups nursed.

When the pups were ten days old, their eyes opened and they sprouted hair. Seven were completely white with pink eyes, like their mother. Two were hooded rats (one of those was Ishbu). Five were black with eyes like tiny jet beads. Frederick was the only lilac rat.

Once the baby rats could eat regular food, they grew quickly. Frederick and Ishbu played rat games all day long with their sisters—tumbling about in their nest, running up ramps, and hiding in the shavings. Their cage was filled with the happy sounds of gnawing, hissing, and squeaking. When the babies were tired, they curled up together and slept soundly, nose to tail. Life was good.

Then one night Igor got out of his tank.

Earlier that evening, as usual, the pet shop owner had switched off the lights and locked the front door. The bell on the door jingled as he closed it. The shop was dark except for the streetlight outside, which shone through the front window blinds, casting striped shadows on the floor.

The rat pups slept peacefully in their cage, their ears like tiny rose petals, their eyes shut tight.

Igor nudged the lid of his tank. Perhaps the shop clerk had not fastened it correctly. Or perhaps Igor had taught himself how to open the cage. In any case the lock gave way with a sharp snap, and the dry rustle of scales filled the shop as Igor slithered out.

He slid up the heating duct. Every animal in the shop heard the shuffle of scales across the shelves, the faint hiss as Igor used his tongue to smell the air. Every animal's head went up, whiskers, tails, ears alert. Danger! Danger!

"Lissssten up," Igor hissed. "I am your ssssovereign. I am your czzzar. I am kissssmet. I demand a sssacrifice."

The hamsters and guinea pigs, the mice and kittens, the puppies, bunnies, turtles, geckos, iguanas, and smaller snakes shook in their cages. Every animal had heard stories of the Nightmare King who resided in the largest tank in the darkest, farthest corner of the pet shop.

And now the nightmare was real.

Igor dropped from the heating duct and wound

around the shelf holding the first row of cages and tanks. One by one he slipped the latches, slithering and sliding down the shelves until every cage door hung open. Then he coiled up on the top shelf and wove his heavy head back and forth, back and forth, surveying his kingdom through scaled eyes.

"I am your sssssovereign. I am your czzzzar. I demand a sssacrifice."

The hypnotic rhythm of his voice cast a spell on the animals. They crept out and lined up on the shop floor beneath the swaying snake.

Frederick and Ishbu were the last to arrive. They'd been sound asleep, curled up against each other. They stumbled into the ranks behind their sisters and mother.

Igor peered down and considered his prey. Was he hungry enough for a puppy? Maybe that curly-haired black-and-white terrier? He could crush it in the rolls of his lithe, muscular body and swallow it whole.

But the shop owner had fed him a live chicken only three nights ago, and he was not hungry enough for puppies or bunnies. Of course he didn't really do this for hunger. He did it for power. Like any tyrant, he fed on fear. He did it to show that he could.

A kitten then? Maybe the pretty Siamese with the clear blue eyes? "Ssssiamese," he called. "Ssssstep forward." The kitten padded toward him, her blue eyes unseeing. Igor's tongue flicked in and out. On the floor the other animals stayed in their ranks, mesmerized.

No, not a kitten. Too squishy. And mice were too little—more appetizer than meal. Guinea pigs were too furry—their long coats gave him heartburn for days. With a casual nod he dismissed the kittens, bunnies, guinea pigs, and tiny white mice; and they filed back to their cages like sleepwalkers. With a flick of his tongue he also excused the lizards, geckos, turtles, and toads. Too bulky. Too cold.

Igor gazed down at his remaining selection—the rows of hamsters and rats standing as silent as tombstones.

"Sssso, which will it be?" He looked at the rats. "Jussst the right amount of meat on your bonesss." He imagined the delightful sound of those bones crunching as he squeezed the coils of his body until the puny heart stopped. He shuddered with pleasure, and his scales rustled again.

On the shop floor Frederick shuddered too. He was not in a trance like the other animals. Ishbu's eyes were glazed like doughnuts, but for some reason Igor's hypnotic weaving didn't work on Frederick. Maybe because, even at that young age, he was unusually determined. Whatever the reason, Frederick remained awake.

He pretended, so he wouldn't attract Igor's attention. But as brave as he was, he was also afraid.

Igor uncoiled and slithered down the shelves as if there were an elevator—top shelf, going down; fourth shelf, going down; third shelf; second shelf; floor.

Frederick wanted to run, to hide. But what would happen to his family if he did?

Igor ignored the hamsters, who didn't move. "A delicioussss rat. A ssspicy and toothsssome rat. That'ssss what I will have. Ssssstep forward, ratsssss, and let me sssssssmell you."

The rats stepped forward as one, their tiny paws echoing on the cold floor. Except Ishbu, whose trance was now so deep that he fell forward, and he lay spread out like a fur rug. Igor spotted him instantly and slithered forward, his massive body brushing past Frederick, who was still pretending to be hypnotized.

"Yessssss, thissss one will do nicely. Jusssst right." Igor smiled, winding his coils around Ishbu.

THE DANCE OF DEATH

FEW RAT PUPS COULD HAVE DONE what Frederick did next.

He ran up to the huge snake and bit Igor right through the tough brown and green scales of his back. If Frederick had been a full-grown rat he might have caused real damage, perhaps killed Igor. But his baby teeth barely punctured Igor's skin. Still the snake stopped squeezing Ishbu and looked at Frederick's whiskery face inches from his own.

"Ssssso, you want to play, do you? A little exersss-size before dinner? Fine. I'll come back for ssssupper later."

Frederick leaped out of the way before the snake could strike. He dashed up the nearest set of shelves. Igor climbed after him, winding his immense body around and around the shelf support, pushing his way up with his rippling muscles. He moved surprisingly fast for such a large animal.

Frederick balanced on the top shelf. He leaned down. Igor was coming up fast. "Wake up!" he shouted to his rat family on the floor below. "Wake up!" he urged the hamsters, standing silently in their ranks. "Run!" he shouted. "Now is your chance! Run! Hide!" Not one eyelid flickered. Not one muscle twitched.

The snake was almost upon him. He knew he couldn't outrun Igor. And then who would stop the Nightmare King from killing all the animals? He needed a plan.

Frederick hadn't been to Miss Dove's fifth-grade classroom yet, hadn't begun his education. So what he did next was either sheer dumb luck or the instinct of a clever mind.

He climbed the wires fastened to the wall and leaped from there onto one of the star-shaped sprinkler heads hanging from the ceiling. He gripped it tightly, panting. The sprinkler swayed slightly under his weight. He gnawed through the wires, hoping he would be quick enough. Igor closed in, hauling himself up to the last shelf.

The soft rubber covering broke beneath Frederick's teeth. There was a pop, and a blue flash as the copper wires touched.

Suddenly it rained.

The fire alarm went off. Sprinklers sprayed water

throughout the shop in a heavy, wet mist that drenched Frederick and momentarily blinded Igor.

The rain woke the rats and hamsters. They blinked in the downpour and then scurried off to their cages to hide in their tubes and wheels and under their pine shavings. Frederick watched Ishbu and the rest of his family race back to their cage.

But Igor was not finished. "You will pay for thissss, you foolissssh little rat," he hissed. He was within striking distance. Frederick saw his eyes, flat as arrowheads. The thick head, the flicking tongue, the wicked teeth. Closer and closer he slid.

Frederick's heart pounded like a tiny drum. Every fiber of his being was electrified. He gathered his last ounce of strength and courage, and he jumped from his perch all the way down to the floor.

It was like flying without a landing pad. Diving without water. Falling without a net. Air rushed past his ears and pain stabbed through one of his paws as he hit. He limped to his cage and pulled the door shut behind him.

Igor had never been cheated out of his prey before. As Frederick trembled in the cage with his family, he knew that they were not really safe. He knew, as clearly as if he could read Igor's evil mind, that the boa was coming for him. The Nightmare King would open the cage, thrust his head inside, and swallow every last rat. Whole.

But just then the pet shop owner opened the door and switched on the lights. He found water streaming everywhere, the fire alarm screaming, Igor coiled around the shelf, and all the cages unlocked. The last thing Frederick heard before he passed out from the pain in his paw was the pet shop owner on the phone: "Is this the Fandango Traveling Circus? I have a boa constrictor for you. Free. Pick him up tonight."

Frederick was the hero of the pet shop! But he didn't get to enjoy his fame long, because the next day Miss Dove came in and purchased two rats for her fifth-grade classroom.

FISHBONE MOLLY, THE TERROR OF THE SEA

NOW FOR HOW THIS HISTORY relates to poor Frederick and Ishbu pinned helplessly beneath the paws of the *General Custer*'s cat:

Mangy fur stuck up around the cat's head. Its torn ear was ruffled like a lettuce leaf. One eye blazed blue, but the skin flaps of its empty eye socket were sewn shut with coarse black thread. Each paw holding Frederick and Ishbu captive had six toes, each toe tipped with a lethal claw.

"Shiver me timbers!" cried the cat hoarsely. "What have we here? Rats on me fine vessel?" The cat dangled Ishbu by the tail while keeping its other paw firmly on Frederick. "Rat! Prepare to meet yer maker!"

Cats like to play with their food to work up an appetite and to give their prey a sporting chance. Under the usual circumstances Frederick and

Ishbu might have been able to escape while the cat toyed with them. But a ship's cat has the job of keeping the vessel free of rats, and doing the job as speedily as possible. There'd be no second chance.

Frederick wriggled around like an eel and bit the cat on its leg as hard as he could.

The cat nearly dropped Ishbu in surprise. "Need a lesson, landlubber?" the cat asked, picking up Frederick and dangling both rats by their tails. Frederick squirmed and twisted, but he couldn't get close enough to bite again.

"I was savin' ye for dessert, but I guess I'll eat ye both now. Two for the price o' one," said the cat with a shrug. "Down the hatch, laddies."

The cat closed its blue eye and opened its mouth. Frederick and Ishbu hung over the yawning cavern. Closer and closer came the slimy tongue, the foul cat breath, and the jagged teeth shining like stalagmites and stalactites in a red cave.

Just as the cat was about to drop the rat brothers into its mouth, the single eye opened and stared at Frederick.

"Bless me ears and whiskers! If it ain't the great lilac rat, the hero o' the pet shop!"

The cat set Frederick and Ishbu down on the floor of the dark little room but kept its paw on their tails so they couldn't run away.

"Don't ye know me, mateys?" asked the cat.

"Fishbone Molly! I was but a wee kitten then and nearly snake bait. Ye saved my life—and that o' me littermates, me mum and dad, and every last critter in the pet shop!"

Frederick looked at the huge, mangy Siamese cat. There was no trace of a sweet little kitten in the big, scarred face. No trace—except one clear blue eye.

Ishbu sat up and opened his eyes, relieved that they were not about to be eaten. He cleared his throat several times. "Very nice to see you again," he finally said. "Fishbone Molly, did you say? We're Ishbu and Frederick. Frederick is the brave one," he added.

Fishbone Molly released their tails and touched whiskers with the rat brothers. Frederick held his breath. He didn't like being this close to a cat, even one who claimed to be friendly.

After the introductions Ishbu said, "We're a long way from the pet shop. Water under the bridge and all that. Tell us, how did you end up as a ship's cat?"

The cat grinned. "That's a whale o' a tale, mateys, indeed it is." She polished her face with her paw. "Make yerselves at home."

The rats sat back and listened.

"I was purchased by a spinster lady who took me home to her wee cottage. A saucer o' milk every day and a tidbit o' tuna on Sundays. Peace and quiet. A life o' ease!" The cat spat. "That wouldn't do for the likes o' me! She expected me to sit by the fire and purr! But me adventurous nature demanded more excitement, so I ran away to sea.

"As fortune would have it, the first ship I sailed on was captured by pirates. 'Moll,' said Cap'n Hawk, 'I need a good mouser, for I'm sore fed up with rats. Join up with us or walk the plank!'

"So I joined 'em. I sailed the seven seas for a year and a day, over the bounding Spanish Main and along the Barbary Coast, and I've lived to tell the tale. I lost me eye in a mighty battle in the Caribbean and the tip o' me ear to a shark in the Indian Ocean. Aye! Those were the days!" Fishbone Molly closed her good eye and purred.

"And I've not regretted a minute of it!" she announced, skewering the rat brothers with her fierce blue glare. "But bad luck and bad times have hounded me these many years. At long last I've come aboard the *General Custer*, and a sorrier ship I've never set sail on. Soon as we hit port, I'm shipping out on a new vessel. But tell me now—how do two brave rats like yerselves happen to be sailing on the *Custer*?"

Ishbu, friendly and trusting as ever, told her about their adventures since the pet shop—including the Big Cheese, the Burmese Bandicoot, and their escape from the Bilgewater Brigade.

Fishbone Molly rubbed her ear with her paw.

"Sorry to break it to ye, mates, but ye've jumped from the frying pan into the stew. The crew of the *Custer* is as motley a mess o' cutthroats, villains, and black-hearted knaves as ye'll ever meet!"

MOLLY MAKES A PLAN

FREDERICK AND ISHBU STARED at Fishbone Molly in horror. Now they knew why the wharf rats had laughed when they'd jumped aboard!

But the cat winked. "Never fear, me hearties! Ye've got Fishbone Molly on yer side! I've never let a friend down yet. I hate these poxy lubbers who call themselves seamen. We'll twiddle their whiskers all right!"

Frederick watched Molly. She was, after all, a pirate cat; and pirates weren't noted for honesty. How could he tell whether she would help them or turn them over to the crew?

Ishbu had no such worries. "Good!" he said. He wiped his nose and sleeked back his whiskers. "And after that can we have breakfast?"

Molly gave a hearty chuckle. "Follow me," she said. She led them out of the room, through a door they hadn't noticed before.

"Stay close," she whispered. They sneaked down a narrow passageway to the galley, where they raided the trash cans.

Later, stuffed with fish skins and orange peels, they followed Molly back to the storage room. "Yer safest here," she said. "If the crew catches sight o' ye, the jig's up. I'll be back at dawn, and we'll make our plan to outwit these scurvy knaves and jump ship."

"But Molly!" cried Ishbu. "I can't swim!"

Fishbone Molly grinned. "It's just my manner o' speaking. Not a hair on yer hide will suffer salt-water. Count on me."

After Molly left, Ishbu and Frederick huddled in the dark, sneezing a little from the cat fur. They had never spent so much time with a cat, and it was a bit overpowering.

"Can we trust her, Freddy?" whispered Ishbu, not so trusting after all.

"What choice do we have?" Frederick said. "We can't sail, and even I can't swim that far. There's no way to get off this ship before we reach port. Until then we'd better do what she says and hope for the best."

Hours passed. The brothers were dry, if not warm; and Ishbu's seasickness had indeed improved. Ishbu slept and Frederick worried, as usual, nibbling his toenails practically down to the bone.

Suddenly the door creaked open, and a slender ribbon of light spread across the floor.

A VIEW FROM
THE BRIDGE

WHEN THE DOOR OPENED, ISHBU squeaked in fright and Frederick crouched, ready to run; but it was only Fishbone Molly coming back. She had mastered the technique of hooking the door open by curling her paw underneath it.

"Psst," she whispered in her hoarse voice. "Follow me."

She led them into the passageway, which was too bright to suit Frederick. He and Ishbu crept close to the wall, following Molly through the passages of the ship and up a narrow flight of stairs. At last they came to a steel door. Molly hooked it with her paw, and the door creaked open. It was the bridge.

Frederick knew a ship's bridge didn't span a river—it was a room above the deck where the controls for the ship were located. Still, he could hardly take it in when the three animals sneaked inside.

He was actually standing on the bridge! His eyes shone with excitement.

The bridge was lit only by the dim green lights of the instrument panel. Through the windows, the animals could see the chill light of dawn streaking the edge of the eastern sea. The motion of the ship was stronger. Ishbu's stomach rolled as the ship rose up and plunged down. The wind whistled around the windows.

"In for a bit of a blow, I fear," rasped Molly.

A man smelling of tobacco snored noisily in a chair in the corner. A trickle of brown drool dribbled down his chin. Fishbone Molly looked at him and spat.

"Lazy son of a sea cook." She leaned over to the rats. "I told you it was a scurvy-dog ship. Badly run and badly crewed." She shook her head. "Cap'n Hawk would never have stood for the likes o' this."

She led the way across the floor to a table. Partly hidden beneath the table was a cardboard box. "Hop in," she whispered. "The captain and first mate will be here soon."

She jumped lightly into the box. Ishbu scrambled up after her and tumbled inside. It was evidently a favorite spot of hers. A tattered burlap bag made a cushiony pillow. Molly turned around three times before lying down, tucking her forelegs beneath her. Ishbu settled in next to her, stirring up a drift of cat hair. He sneezed.

Frederick looked around. The box was a perfect place to eavesdrop, concealed from any humans. But he wasn't ready to hide, not yet. The sailor looked safely asleep, and now might be his only chance to see a ship's bridge in action!

Frederick climbed up to the control panel. It glowed with all sorts of dials, gauges, and instruments. He was fascinated, though he didn't know what any of them did. (Miss Dove hadn't covered that.) Even more fascinating were the charts and maps stacked up on the table, and he jumped across to examine them more closely.

A dusty, old-fashioned globe stood on one side as though it had been set there by someone long ago and forgotten. The globe reminded Frederick of class, and a small lump formed in his throat. If Miss Dove could only see him now!

Fishbone Molly was right; they didn't have long to wait. The door banged open, and two men strode inside.

"Rats!" cried one of the men.

AN UNCHARTED ISLAND

 FREDERICK DIDN'T HAVE TIME TO jump into Molly's box. He scrunched down behind the globe and tried to make himself as small as possible.

"What's that, Mr. Stimms?" one of the men said.

"I saw something move. A rat maybe. I hates rats."

"You're blind as a bat, Mr. Stimms. There's no rat."

Frederick peeked around the globe. The shorter man wore a cap with a shiny black brim trimmed in gold braid. Frederick decided he must be the captain. The man's round face was as seamed and scarred as an old wooden oar.

The tall, thin man, who must have been the first mate, had a blue knit cap pulled low over his brow. His nose jutted out like a ship's prow, and his chin disappeared into the neck of his sweater like a turtle into its shell.

The captain caught sight of the sailor still sleeping in the corner. "Get off your duff, you lazy swab," he said, kicking the sailor in the leg.

The sailor jumped to his feet, rubbing his eyes.

"Set a course south, full speed ahead," barked the captain.

"Aye, aye, sir!" The sailor saluted and went to the wheel.

"But Cap'n, ain't we gonna put in at Calcutta and off-load our cargo?" asked the skinny first mate.

"When I want your advice, Mr. Stimms, I'll ask for it. Give me that chart."

Frederick scrunched down even more as Mr. Stimms grabbed the chart from a stack near his hiding place. The captain spread the map out on the table and leaned over it. Frederick strained to see, but he could not make out the markings.

"Blimey," muttered the captain, tapping his fingers on the chart. He lowered his voice so the sailor wouldn't overhear. "A secret island! I've sailed these seas all me life and never heard of it." He took off his cap and scratched his head. "Well, it's a simple enough job from the looks of it. Go in, pick up the statue, and get out. Then we'll off-load this fertilizer in Calcutta; load jute for New Orleans. After that we'll deliver the statue to its new owner."

Frederick's fur prickled. A statue! Could it be?

Mr. Stimms ran a weathered hand over his face. "They say it's worth millions. But that ain't all. They say it's cursed."

"Getting superstitious on me?" The captain glowered.

"What do you suppose he wants it for?" asked Mr. Stimms. "He don't need the money."

"Who cares? What he does with it is his own business."

"You ever seen him?" Mr. Stimms asked curiously.

The captain shook his head. "No need, as long as he pays." He used his sleeve to polish a dial on the instrument panel. "We communicate with codes. We don't see him, he don't see us. Everybody's happy."

Beyond the windows, Frederick watched the sun rise, staining the dark clouds red, turning the sea the color of blood. Waves crashed over the deck railing. The ship pitched like a rocking horse.

"Red sky at morning, sailors take warning," said the sailor.

The captain ignored him. "Mind you follow the map," he told the first mate. "The Burmese Bandicoot is hidden on an uncharted island—uncharted that is except for this, the only map in existence, come to us from our mysterious employer."

They were after the Burmese Bandicoot! Frederick's eyes widened.

The captain pointed to the map again, and this time Frederick could just make out a large red *X* drawn on the chart.

"There is a strong current along the west coast," murmured the captain. "Better steer clear of that. But there's a reef to the south. We'll anchor off here." He pointed to a spot on the chart. "And take the dinghy in."

"And—your pardon, sir—what do I tell the crew about our unscheduled stop?" asked Mr. Stimms.

The captain scowled. "Tell 'em there's double pay for those that can keep their mouths shut. And Davy Jones's locker for them that can't!"

X MARKS THE SPOT

BEHIND THE GLOBE, FREDERICK's pulse quickened. An uncharted island! Miss Dove had taught her fifth graders how to remember the seven continents of the world. <u>A</u>unt <u>A</u>bby <u>N</u>ever <u>S</u>aw <u>A</u>n <u>E</u>lephant <u>A</u>ct: Asia, Africa, North America, South America, Antarctica, Europe, and Australia.

The four major oceans were easy to remember too. <u>P</u>olly <u>A</u>te <u>I</u>sabel's <u>A</u>pple: Pacific, Atlantic, Indian, and Arctic.

But Frederick didn't know where the secret island was—the mysterious island that hid the Burmese Bandicoot.

He had to get another look at that map!

It seemed to take forever for the captain and Mr. Stimms to exit the bridge. Finally they left, banging the door behind them. Rain spattered the windows. The sailor stood at his post for a while longer, staring out at the threatening clouds scudding across the sky and the dirty seas rising before them. Then he yawned, sat down in the chair, and went back to sleep.

Frederick ran lightly across the table and peered at the chart. A treasure map! Just like the ones in the great books Miss Dove had read to her class: *Treasure Island, Robinson Crusoe,* and *The Hardy Boys and the Secret of Pirates' Hill*!

Frederick looked at the compass rose. "Never Eat Soggy Worms," he softly repeated. "North, East, South, West." He made a mental note that the island was south of the continent of Asia, in the Indian Ocean. He found India, and Calcutta, the port for which they were headed next. If only he could find out their current position!

Fishbone Molly squinted up at him from her box. Her whiskers bristled. "Ahoy! Back to the storage room, me hearties. We'd best be making plans."

Ishbu climbed out of the box and followed her to the door. Frederick jumped off the table, and as silently as thieves, the three animals sped down the corridor to the storage room.

They were so excited that they hardly noticed how much the pitch and roll of the ship had increased.

Fishbone Molly opened the door. Once inside she turned to the rats, her eye glittering like a sapphire in the dim light. She purred. "Did ye hear that, mates? Yer Burmese Bandicoot! Oh, this be a job for Fishbone Molly, terror o' the seas!"

She pulled the rats so close that her whiskers tickled. "We'll let the cap'n find the statue on the island, and then *we'll* steal it from *him* before we reach Calcutta! Join me, mates, and we'll go halves! It's Fate's hand at work!"

Before Frederick could speak, Ishbu said, "No thanks. Not this rat. I'm for home and Miss Dove's classroom lickety-split. No more oceans or ships or villains or adventures for me!"

"But Ishbu," pleaded Frederick. "The statue is so close. Molly's right—this is meant to be. Why else would we keep stumbling across it? It's an adventure. *Our* adventure!"

Ishbu's usually happy face narrowed in a stubborn frown. "No, Frederick. I told you before. I'm not going on a treasure hunt. I want to go home."

Frederick tried one more time. "But Ishbu, we can't go back to Miss Dove's class. What about Millicent Mallory? And Kay Serah and Mr. Stern? If we go back we'll be exterminated!" Frederick nibbled Ishbu's neck encouragingly, but Ishbu pulled away.

Fishbone Molly interrupted: "And if ye stay on board, ye'll be exterminated as well. Lazy the crew may be, but they've got strict rules to de-rat before putting in to port. There'll be poison and traps everywhere in a few days; and if that don't do the trick, the cap'n will have the ship fumigated in Calcutta."

Frederick wasn't entirely sure what *fumigated* meant, but he knew it was bad. He looked at Molly, his whiskers drooping. It suddenly occurred to him that Fishbone Molly was the only one who knew they were on board. Would she threaten to betray them to the crew unless they helped her steal the statue?

But Molly wasn't interested in blackmail. She winked her one blue eye. "Sorry ye won't join up with me," she told the brothers. "We would have had a high ol' time. But more booty for me if I'm working alone. I'll help ye escape this ship just the same before we reach port. No hard feelings."

Once again the tantalizing prospect of adventure and riches floated out of Frederick's reach.

"All right, Ishbu," he said reluctantly. "We can't go back to W. H. E. S. But maybe we can find a home somewhere else."

"Somewhere safe? With marshmallow treats? And carrot sticks? And a warm nest of shredded paper?" Ishbu added wistfully, brushing his paws over his moist eyes. "A home for us?"

Frederick nodded. *A home somewhere with a teacher like Miss Dove,* he thought. Somewhere with books and maps and globes, somewhere he could dream about adventures, travel, and geography.

Ishbu clicked his teeth happily. "Thanks, Freddy!"

The next second they were flying through the air as a tremendous explosion rocked the ship.

RATS (AND CAT) DESERT A SINKING SHIP

 FREDERICK STAGGERED TO HIS feet and shook his head to clear it. Crashes, roars, and booms echoed throughout the ship. *A-OO-GAAA!* blared the horn. Feet pounded down the passage outside the storage room. With all the noise the rats didn't notice that the thrumming engines had fallen silent.

"What's happening?" yelled Ishbu.

"Beats me," cried Fishbone Molly. "But it sure as tootin' ain't good!"

The captain's voice bellowed over the intercom: "All hands on deck!"

"C'mon!" growled Molly. She sped through the passageway and up the narrow stairs. Sailors sprinted past but paid no attention either to the mangy old mouser or the two rats racing along behind her.

They slipped through the door behind a sailor and out on to the open deck, taking shelter beneath a coil of rope. Black clouds whipped across the sky. Rain battered the deck like a thousand hammers. Enormous waves crashed over the bulwarks. The wind tore at their fur.

Men in yellow oilskins ran all around them, shouting. Thick smoke boiled out of the hold. "Fire in the hold! Fire in the hold!" came a panicked cry. The captain stood on the deck above them scowling at his frantic crew.

"Man the pumps!" he yelled.

"She's dead in the water!" a sailor hollered back.

"She's foundering!" cried another.

Ishbu, Frederick, and Fishbone Molly cowered in the shelter of the rope. Water swirled around their paws. "What's happening?" Ishbu yelled again.

Fishbone Molly's whiskers bent back in the wind. "The cargo! I'd bet the fertilizer blew up in the hold! It's explosive."

The ship groaned and settled to starboard, listing dangerously close to the surging gray water. The rat brothers clung to each other, shivering with fear, but Molly grinned, her torn ear fluttering like a flag. No fears for a pirate cat.

"If she's dead in the water, she can't be steered," Molly shouted over the howl of the wind. "She'll roll in this surf and sink. Let's get out while the getting's good. Quick, follow me!"

"But I can't swim!" yelled Ishbu.

"Prepare to abandon ship!" ordered the captain.

The Siamese cat and the rats took to their paws, racing across the deck to the ship's rail. Far below them a lifeboat danced on the waves like a racehorse waiting for the starting gate to lift. Three sailors prepared to lower another.

"That's for us!" yelled Fishbone Molly. "Jump!" She sprang to the rail and balanced. Then, with a powerful push of her hind legs, she shoved off. Frederick braced himself against the wind, watching anxiously. Molly landed on her feet in the first lifeboat. She peered up at the rats through the driving rain and waved her tail before she dodged beneath a sheltering tarp.

"Let's go!" yelled Frederick. "Quick, before the next wave!"

The ship rose up and up, climbing a wall of water as steep as a mountain. The *Custer* teetered on the crest and plunged down, down, down like a roller coaster.

"Watch out!" yelled Frederick.

A gigantic wave broke over the ship and swept across the deck. Two sailors lost their balance, and the lifeboat they had been trying to lower flipped and capsized into the briny deep.

Frederick was knocked off his feet. He swirled

across the deck on a surge of icy green water and slammed against the rail. He caught it and clung with every bit of his strength, coughing and sputtering, shaking the stinging saltwater out of his eyes. He lashed his tail around the railing and held on tight.

Ishbu was swept up also but had no chance to grab anything. He paddled fiercely with his tiny paws, but the current was too strong. He was sucked through the scupper and into the sea.

LOST AT SEA

 WHAT IS THE BIGGEST DANGER IN being swept overboard in a typhoon? It's hard to choose. There's drowning, of course. Or being eaten by sharks—certainly a gruesome and painful death. Dying of hypothermia, which occurs when the body becomes too cold. Or of dehydration when there is no fresh water to drink.

How could Ishbu survive all these dangers?

None of the busy sailors noticed a lone rat swept out to sea. There was no one to cry, "Rat overboard!" No one to throw him a life preserver.

Frederick, from his desperate hold on the ship's railing, was the only one who saw his brother washed overboard. "Ishbu!" he howled. "Ishbu!" But there was nothing he could do. He could only watch helplessly as Ishbu's tiny, limp body sank beneath the waves.

Meanwhile, the rain still poured from the skies, drenching Frederick's fur, pounding the deck. The wind roared like a demon. The ship groaned and settled lower into the water.

The next wave will swamp us, worried Frederick.

Waves surged across the deck. Frederick's paws were so cold they turned blue.

I can't hold on any longer, he thought, *I really can't.*

Just then a barrel floated across the deck below him, bobbing in the swirl of water.

It was an old wooden barrel, the kind pirates used to keep rum in, not the sort of thing you'd expect on a modern ship. But it was lucky for Frederick it showed up. Always one to seize opportunity, he let go of the railing and dropped onto the barrel. He dug his claws into the wood and held on with all his might.

As he feared, the next wave swamped the ship. The remaining sailors jumped into the lifeboats. The wave lifted Frederick's barrel over the railing and swept it out into the angry, gray sea.

The wind howled; the rain battered Frederick like spray from a fire hose; the waves rose and fell in mighty hills and valleys. Frederick clung to the barrel like a bronco rider in a rodeo. Twice the barrel spun completely upside down, and Frederick went with it, right into the water, and came up choking and sputtering. He wrapped his tail around the barrel hoop.

The violent storm swept him far, far away from the sinking ship. The lifeboats were out of sight. All Frederick's concentration was on staying upright and staying afloat, so he barely noticed when the storm weakened. The wind died down to a steady roar, and the rain pelted but did not drench.

Fishbone Molly was gone. He hoped she would make it in her lifeboat. Since it was Molly, he was pretty sure she would. But Ishbu was gone without a fighting chance. Frederick thought of his brother sinking beneath the waves.

He threw his head up and howled. But his tears were just tiny drops of water in the vastness of the ocean.

"WATER, WATER, EVERYWHERE . . ."

 EXHAUSTED, FREDERICK PASSED out. When he opened his eyes, the storm had passed. He was drifting alone in a blue bowl. The sea and sky melded together until it was hard to tell up from down—sparkling water below him, a misty horizon, and overhead, a turquoise sky.

He tried to sit. The wooden barrel wobbled, and Frederick moved carefully so he wouldn't be spilled into the briny deep. He unwound his tail and rubbed it tenderly. His tongue had swelled, and his mouth and throat were so dry that it was hard to swallow. His fur was stiff with dried saltwater. His eyes burned in the heat and glare of the sun.

The barrel bobbed like a cork in a bathtub. Frederick shaded his eyes with his paws and stared at the horizon. Nothing. Not a ship, not a cloud, not a landfall. The seascape was empty. Just one lost, weary rat on a barrel floating alone in the Indian Ocean.

He lay back down and put his paws over his eyes. He knew that getting drinking water was the highest priority. He could live without food for a while—not long though, because rats are small and don't have much body fat—but he absolutely couldn't survive without water.

So he must get some. But how? Seawater was too salty. It would only make him thirstier. He limply trailed one paw in the ocean.

"'Water, water, everywhere, nor any drop to drink'!" In spite of his weariness, his fear, his grief over Ishbu, his whiskers curled up a little bit. It wasn't every rat who could quote Samuel Taylor Coleridge!

He shot up, nearly capsizing his frail craft. It wouldn't help anything to keep lying here like a sunbather on a beach. He had survived the sinking ship and the typhoon. Now he must survive to find Ishbu!

But was there any way that Ishbu could have weathered the great storm? He didn't even have a life jacket. Frederick lay back down again and used up some of his precious body water in tears.

Even the bravest rats cry sometimes.

After a while Frederick began to feel hungry, so he nibbled on the wooden slats of the barrel. Rats can eat nearly anything—garbage, soap, the plastic tubing on electric wires—so the wood of the barrel was like popcorn to Frederick, pleasantly chewy and satisfying. He was careful not to chew a hole clear through. He didn't want to sink!

After eating, Frederick felt well enough to sit up. The sun beat down mercilessly, and he wished he had some way of covering his head. He scanned the ocean in case someone or something useful floated past.

The water was so clear, he could see down a few feet. A shadow drifted by. It was a bit of tangled fishing line. Frederick scooped it up. It was obviously too thin to provide any relief from the sun, but it might come in handy. He tied it to the barrel hoop.

The next thing to float by was more useful. A glass soda bottle! He could use it to collect rainwater—*if* it rained. The brand name was in a foreign language, but Frederick recognized the red-and-white logo. It was heavy, and he nearly rolled off the barrel trying to grab it, but he managed. The underside was covered in large barnacles. The bottle must have drifted for ages.

Frederick quickly broke off a barnacle and sucked out the juice. At once he felt more hopeful. After all, there was no need to despair completely. He'd read that castaways sometimes drifted for thousands of miles before reaching land. All he had to do was stay alive, and surely he would wash up along some coast or be rescued by a passing ship. Just remember Robinson Crusoe! Remember the Swiss Family Robinson!

Several hours later a piece of flotsam raised his spirits even more. A foot or so of black, plastic garbage sack floated by like an oil slick. Frederick grabbed it and hauled it aboard his craft. It would make a sunshade and hopefully decrease his chances of dehydration. He draped it over his head and immediately felt cooler.

The barrel spun faster in the water. The piece of garbage sack flapped in the wind, and Frederick had trouble holding it. He coiled his tail around the bottle and held the sack with both paws so that it wouldn't blow away. The wind caught the plastic and pushed the barrel, almost like . . . a sail!

Frederick's forelegs grew tired and achy from holding the sack, but it gave him an idea. If only he had a mast!

As evening came, the plastic sack became too hard to hold against the stiffening breeze. Frederick folded it up. The sun was dropping below the horizon anyway and no longer beat down upon his poor head.

He straightened out the fishing line and used it like a rope to lash the bottle and plastic sack securely to his barrel. He didn't want to lose any of his treasures. Perhaps in the morning he would find a stick or piece of wood to use as a mast.

The night was incredibly beautiful. The air was warm, and a soft breeze ruffled his fur. Stars blazed in the sky, constellations he'd heard of but had never seen. A school of flying fish leaped over his barrel, sprinkling him with water drops that sparkled like diamonds in the starlight.

Miss Dove had said that the mariners of old had steered by the stars. *Maybe I could do that,* he thought. *I could probably do that.*

Just before he fell asleep he again felt the sharp stab of Ishbu's absence. How Ishbu would have loved seeing the flying fish! How he would have loved eating barnacles!

"Ishbu, my brother," whispered Frederick. "I hope you are at peace."

THE LONELY SEA

 THE NEXT DAY FREDERICK BROKE his fast with barnacle juice and wood gnawed from the barrel. He felt stronger and more optimistic. If he could sail his tiny vessel, he could find land. If he could find land, he could survive.

But first he needed to find a mast.

It took all day—a long, hot, boring day in which he did nothing but drift. His paws grew weary from holding up the plastic sunshade; his eyes grew tired of staring, staring out to sea. But at last his effort was rewarded—a long stick drifted within reach, and he grabbed it.

It was too long to be a mast. Disappointed, he nearly threw it overboard before he realized—his teeth! He chewed the stick into two pieces and saved the shorter half. A castaway couldn't afford to waste anything!

The longer end would make a sturdy mast. He gnawed a small hole in the barrel, plugged it with a bit of the plastic so water couldn't get inside, and shoved in the mast. It stood up straight and true. As straight and true as a piece of driftwood could, at any rate.

He bit a row of tiny holes in a piece of the plastic and laced the fishing line through it for rigging. He tied it to his mast. The sail fluttered and flapped. He drew it taut with the line. The sail bellied out with the freshening breeze, and the little barrel skimmed over the waves like a water bug.

Now, if only I had a rudder, I could steer. I could navigate by the stars, the way the ancients did. His mind filled with visions of the Phoenicians, the Vikings, and the Egyptians.

At dusk he dined again on barnacles and wood. It was rapidly becoming a boring diet. *Maybe I can catch a fish,* he thought. *Tomorrow I can make a fishing line. And a hat and sunglasses. . . .* He fell asleep making plans, and dreaming of Ishbu.

Morning brought his first visitor. A large gray fin broke through the water beside the barrel. Frederick sat up, his heart thudding in his chest—shark!

But then he realized that the fin was curved, not triangular; and the eye was large and liquid, not flat and cold like the eye of a shark. A dolphin!

Frederick remembered stories he'd heard about

helpful dolphins, even a famous Greek story about a boy who was towed to shore by holding on to a dolphin's fin.

He leaned close to the water and cupped his paws around his snout. "Ahoy, there!" he called. "Can you tell me where the nearest land is?"

But either this wasn't a helpful kind of dolphin or else she thought Frederick had the situation well in paw. She blew a stream of moist air through her blowhole, then dove beneath the barrel and swam away. Frederick could see her sleek shape gliding beneath the surface of the water. He watched her leave with regret. She would have been someone to talk to at least.

He went back to work on his rudder, nibbling the short piece of wood into a triangle and fastening it as well as he could with the last of the fishing line. It was fragile, but it would have to do. He moved it back and forth with satisfaction.

He sailed along. Tonight he'd look for the North Star. Miss Dove had told them how Harriet Tubman had followed the North Star as she led slaves north to freedom.

Maybe he could follow the North Star too.

Of course he was much farther south than Harriet Tubman had been. But if he was somewhere in the Indian Ocean, as he suspected, then land would be due north. If only he'd gotten a better look at the chart on the *General Custer*! Still, it was worth a try.

The night was soft and warm. The stars winked like fireflies in the black velvet sky. Using the Little Dipper as a guide, Frederick located Polaris, another name for the North Star, and set his course. "'All I ask is a tall ship and a star to steer her by,'" he recited softly.

He sailed for many nights, always following the North Star. He grew thin on his diet of barnacles and wood. His coat coarsened beneath the tropical sun. His gums swelled from the lack of vitamins. His paws roughened and split from the saltwater. Nevertheless, it was the most exciting time of his life. Here he was, pitted against the elements! Having adventures—incredible adventures—that rivaled any book's!

Then he would remember that Ishbu wasn't here to share the journey with him, and his heart grew heavy again.

On the tenth day he saw clouds—puffy, white clouds—on the horizon.

That could mean only one thing!

ROUGH LANDING

THERE ARE MANY WAYS A SAILOR can tell that land is nearby before he can actually see it. He might notice land-based seabirds flying overhead or dark seaweed or leaves in the water. Or he might glimpse the distant white line of surf indicating a coral reef, or—like Columbus—he might see the fluffy cumulus clouds that form over land.

Frederick spotted the clouds first, massed on the horizon like a flock of woolly sheep, and beneath them the misty shape of mountains. He gave the age-old cry of sailors: "Land ho!" His voice croaked like a raven's. He adjusted his sail, put his paw on the rudder, and sailed toward the clouds. *If only Ishbu were here!*

Other signs of land came swiftly: the scent of tropical flowers on the breeze, the cry—so long unheard—of seabirds, a coconut bobbing in the water. He sailed his little barrel up each swell and swooshed down.

It took all afternoon, but as the sun began to sink, he saw the dark shapes of mountains and coconut palms silhouetted against the sunset skies. *I shouldn't try to land in the dark*, he reasoned. *It would be too dangerous.* As anxious as he was to be ashore, he couldn't risk the unseen hazards that might wreck his frail craft: riptides, sharp coral reefs, cliffs, breaking surf. In daylight he could scout the coastline until he found a shallow, sloping sandy beach. So he stayed out from the shore a little bit, determined to wait until dawn.

But the decision was torn from his paws.

Surfers say that every tenth wave is the biggest; poets say it is every ninth wave that rolls in higher and stronger than the previous ones. Frederick had not been counting waves. He'd been lowering the sail to wait out beyond the reef until morning when a huge wave—a powerful, rolling wave—curled right up behind him.

Frederick was sucked up the curl. The mountain of water capsized his barrel and tossed him into the raging surf. The wave broke over him, tumbling him like a shirt in a dryer, slamming him across the ocean floor. His mouth filled with water, his nose with sand. The wave swept him up and flung him on the rocks like a piece of flotsam.

He lay on the shore for a moment, coughing up seawater. He heard the hiss of the receding surf. He had to crawl higher on the beach before another wave dragged him out to sea, but his body felt as limp as a noodle. He couldn't move. He *couldn't*.

The waves were coming. He had only seconds to get out of the tide's reach. He was so weakened by his long days at sea, he would have no chance of survival at all if he couldn't get away from the deadly waves.

It was no use. He couldn't force his sunburned paws to pull his body an inch farther, and the relentless sea was coming, coming to claim him. How tragic! To survive the sea only to die on land!

But his fate changed paws again. Two strong ones grabbed his own and hauled him to safety.

CASTAWAY

FREDERICK FELT SOMEONE LIFT him and carry him farther up the beach. Gently he was laid on the sand at the edge of the rocks.

He heard a glad cry—"Freddy!"—and he opened his exhausted eyes to see a familiar figure standing over him.

Ishbu fell to his knees and embraced his brother. "You're alive!" he cried.

"So are you!" Frederick hugged Ishbu with all the strength in his thin, tired forelegs. The rat brothers clicked teeth and touched noses.

"I thought you'd drowned!" Frederick said, his voice still creaky. "How did you . . . How are—"

Ishbu put his paw over Frederick's mouth. "Save your strength. We're going to get you back to the temple." He stared at Frederick's coarse, sun-beaten fur and raw, bleeding paws. "Oh, Freddy!" he cried.

"You're hurt! And so thin! You're nothing but skin and bones!" Tears filled Ishbu's eyes, and he stroked Frederick's fur. "But you're alive!"

Ishbu turned inland and whistled shrilly. At once three sturdy brown rats scampered out of the jungle. They lifted Frederick and carried him up the path into the mangrove trees.

It didn't take long to reach their destination. At the end of the path, lit by the flickering flames of torches, stood the strangest building Frederick had ever seen.

Walls of reddish brown stone were carved all over with exotic designs. Four large, ornamented pillars stood at the corners. Vines grew over the walls. Carved doors—each as tall as five rats standing on one another—hung partly open as if inviting him inside. The entrance was marked with round, white pebbles. A large brass bowl stood near the doors.

"The Secret Temple of Karni Mata," whispered Ishbu.

A night bird cried, and Frederick shivered.

The silver doors opened wide, and the three big rats carried Frederick inside, with Ishbu following, through a courtyard filled with the scent of flowers. Water splashed in a fountain and, somewhere out of sight, a bell chimed softly.

And everywhere there were rats. Frederick could

hear them, smell them, see them scurrying as dusk became dark. The three brown rats walked to the end of the courtyard, through a narrow archway, inside a little room. There they laid Frederick down on a nest of fur and feathers.

"Rest here," said Ishbu. "The priestesses will attend to your wounds and give you food. Then you must sleep." He turned to go.

Frederick reached out a paw. "But Ishbu, don't leave! I want to know how you survived the shipwreck. I saw you washed overboard. I saw you sink beneath the waves! How did you get here? What is this place?"

Ishbu smiled, his plump cheeks narrowing his eyes. "All in good time, dear brother." He patted Frederick's paw. "But now you are tired. You must rest and eat. I will see you at midnight, at the feast."

Ishbu touched Frederick's nose with his own and left the chamber. The other rats bowed low, their whiskers brushing the floor, and then they scampered out after Ishbu, leaving Frederick alone again.

A lantern bathed the small room in gold. The tantalizing scent of curry and coconut wafted to Frederick as he lay on the soft pallet. His stomach growled.

It was only then that Frederick realized how sleek and plump his brother looked. Even more than usual. He didn't look like a castaway at all. And then there were his strange, vague answers.

How had Ishbu survived the shipwreck? Had he been here all this time? And what was this curious place?

DHAVALA

FREDERICK HEARD THE RAT priestesses before he saw them. Tiny squeaks chimed through the courtyard like silver bells. Seven rats entered his chamber, led by an elderly rat as white as moonlight.

"My name is Dhavala," said the old white rat in a low, pleasant tone. "I am the high priestess of Karni Mata, the Mother Goddess. Welcome to her secret temple."

At Dhavala's signal, the priestesses bathed Frederick's wounds in scented oils. They rubbed coconut butter into his raw, swollen paws. They fed him tidbits of curry, bananas, and rice, and gave him coconut milk to drink.

Frederick had never tasted anything so delicious in all his life. But he couldn't seem to nibble more than a few mouthfuls.

"Do not try to eat more," said Dhavala. "Your stomach has shrunk from your days at sea. In time you will heal."

Frederick was very sleepy, but he needed to know more about his surroundings before he could feel safe enough to sleep. "What is this place?" he asked. "Where am I?"

Dhavala's brown eyes shone. Her voice took on a musical lilt. "This is a place known only to rats. Hundreds of years ago, our ancestors left India to build a temple, somewhere they might worship Karni Mata as they pleased.

"They traveled in small boats woven from palm fronds. Their goal was to find an island far away from the affairs of humans. They landed here; and with rat ingenuity, strength, and the blessings of Karni Mata, they built this temple.

"Here all rats are safe. No humans can poison, trap, or exterminate us. No predators can enter our temple grounds: no cats pounce, no snakes squeeze, no owls hunt. Everything we need is here. Our Mother keeps us safe."

Frederick could see that she wore an air of serenity and peace like a cloak.

"Sleep now," she said. "At midnight we will summon you for the feast."

Dhavala left the chamber, followed by the seven priestesses. Frederick's eyes grew heavy as he lay on the bed of fur and feathers. The soft, moist, tropical breeze surrounded him with fragrant, exotic smells—frangipani, coconut, cumin. He closed his eyes and listened to the distant ringing of temple bells and the chatter of the rats in the courtyard. His breathing became slow and steady. At last he slept.

THE LOTUS EATERS

 FREDERICK WAS AWAKENED BY A small brown rat. The rat didn't speak but shook Frederick awake and motioned for him to follow. Frederick padded after him, through the archway and into the moonlit courtyard.

Candles flickered everywhere, giving a warm glow to the tropical night. Frederick heard the hoot of a night bird in the jungle. He shuddered until he remembered Dhavala's words, "No predators can enter." He followed the brown rat over the black and white marble squares of the courtyard and into the great hall.

The walls were hung with panels of pink-and-gold silk. Soft carpets covered the floor. A raised dais stood at the far end of the room with a long wooden table on it.

When Frederick entered, Ishbu stood and

scampered across the floor to touch his brother's nose. "Welcome! Are you rested? Do you feel better?" He led Frederick to the platform. "Sit here, my brother. Tonight we feast. I am so happy you have been spared to share it with us!"

Frederick stared at his brother. Maybe it wasn't his brother at all. Maybe some stranger was pretending to be Ishbu!

He wrinkled his nose and sniffed Ishbu's fur. Nope. Frederick's eyes might deceive him, but his nose never would. It was Ishbu, all right.

"Why are you talking like that?" he asked.

Ishbu laughed. "Sorry, Freddy. It's just that everybody here talks like this. I guess I kind of forgot how I talked before."

"Well, get over it," said Frederick. "You had me worried."

The two rats sat down. Dhavala sat at the head of the table, looking regal and distant. Frederick clicked his teeth to her in greeting, and she nodded back.

There was another rat dining with them, a girl with shiny black eyes and ears like pale pink shells. She had an attractive lilac coat.

"Hello," said Frederick, suddenly shy.

"Natasha," said Ishbu. "I'd like you to meet my brother, Frederick."

Frederick politely sniffed her fur. It held an

appealing cinnamon fragrance. Maybe it was because he'd been so long at sea, but surely this was the prettiest girl rat he'd ever seen!

"You must be telling us all about your adventures," murmured Natasha. Frederick found her Russian accent charming.

The air was filled with the scent of frangipani blossoms. The light from the oil lamps touched everything with a soft warmth. The temple rats served a splendid meal on plaited palm fronds— rice, bamboo shoots, fried cakes, bananas, and curry. Coconut milk slaked their thirst.

While they ate, Frederick told them how he'd built his raft, sail, and rudder and about the long days and nights at sea.

"How amazing!" said Natasha, melting him with a look. "You are very brave and clever rat!"

Frederick blushed. "It wasn't so much. Anyone could have done it." He turned to his brother. "But Ishbu, how did you get here? I thought I'd never see you again!"

Ishbu nodded. "I thought I was a goner for sure. The last things I saw were Fishbone Molly in the lifeboat and you clinging to the ship's railing. Then the wave washed me off the ship and pulled me under. I must have passed out, because the next thing I knew, I was tangled in a bit of fishing net; but instead of pulling me under, the net actually kept me afloat." Ishbu shook his head. "I don't know how."

"Maybe it was held up by fishing floats," suggested Frederick.

Dhavala smiled. "It was the divine intervention of Karni Mata. She keeps her *kabas*, her children, safe."

"Someone must have been looking out for me," Ishbu said, "because that net saved my life again. After the storm was over, a big albatross tried to pick up the net. He must have thought it was a fish. He got caught and tried to fly off with the net hanging from his foot, and me hanging from the net! The weight dragged him down. I thought we'd both drown. Finally I was able to gnaw the net off his foot. To thank me, he dropped me on this island."

Frederick shook his ears. "What incredible adventures you and I have had! Miss Dove would never believe it."

Natasha leaned forward, her eyes very bright. "Tell me," she said, "this ship that sunk—what was her name?"

"The *General Custer*," said Frederick. "An ill-fated name for an ill-fated ship."

Natasha put her paw on his. "And the men on board—the sailors, the captain—all drowned? No one survived?"

"I don't know. I couldn't see much after I jumped on the barrel. The sailors were launching lifeboats. Whether they got safely away . . ." Frederick scratched his chin. "I just don't know."

Ishbu's whiskers drooped. "I sure hope Fishbone Molly made it."

Frederick reassured him. "She's a pirate cat. Brave as any rat. Saltwater runs through her veins. If we came through, I'm sure she did."

"Enough of this sad talk," said Dhavala. She passed Frederick a dish of fried bananas. "You three have survived, you are safe! Let us give our thanks to Karni Mata! Eat, rejoice, and be thankful."

When they had consumed their fill, Dhavala clapped her paws. "Bring on the dancers!" she called.

A group of musicians began to play. Several rats trotted out to the center of the floor and began a whirling, swirling dance. The music grew faster and faster until it made Frederick's head spin. He could hardly keep his eyes open.

"You must get some more sleep," said Ishbu. "It will be daylight soon. Tomorrow night I'll show you around. This is the greatest place ever, Freddy. You're going to love it here."

It wasn't until much later, when Frederick was lying in his nest, that he recalled Dhavala's words: "You *three* have survived."

Frederick ticked them off on the toes of his paw. He was one. Ishbu was two. Two survivors. Who was the third?

THE THIRD SURVIVOR

FREDERICK SLEPT ALL DAY, AS WILD rats do. When the first gold streaks of sunset streamed through the archway, another temple rat arrived to summon him to break his fast. Frederick yawned and stretched, showing his back teeth and sticking out his tongue. He groomed, licked his paws, and sleeked back his whiskers before heading out into the courtyard.

Dusk was falling. The courtyard was filled with soft purple shadows. Brown rats scurried past, bent on ratty errands. For the first time, Frederick noticed little holes all along the base of the raised floor. Rat holes! A tingle raced up his spine. He must explore!

He was sniffing one hole, wondering where it led and if he should crawl inside and find out, when Ishbu came up behind him and playfully nipped

157

him on the tail. "Come on, Freddy! I'm starved! Let's eat. We can explore later."

Frederick scampered along behind Ishbu. "But you've been here a long time. You must have explored it already."

Ishbu scratched. "I looked around some," he said. "And Natasha and I went down some of the tunnels together. But Dhavala says that there are zillions of rat tunnels, secret passages, and hidden rooms. It's like an underground city! A maze!"

Ishbu led the way into the great hall. He and Frederick took their places at the long table. Platters of mango, curry, and sweet sticky rice balls were laid out for all the rats to help themselves. The rat brothers dug in eagerly.

After his good day's sleep, Frederick felt refreshed and lively again. Already his coarse, sun-dried coat was beginning to regain its glossy sheen. His tired, sun-dazzled eyes had stopped burning, and the raw spots on his paws were healing.

Natasha was not there. Frederick found himself watching the arched doorway, hoping to see her.

When she finally entered, his heart gave a little skip. She was so beautiful! Her pale gray coat shone, and her eyes glistened like black pearls. Her elegant, long white whiskers quivered in a most delightful way.

She caught him staring and smiled. Frederick

grew warm. He quickly bent his head and nibbled on the hearts of palm in front of him until he found the courage to look at her again. Any rat might become shy in the presence of such beauty!

He cleared his throat. "I hope you slept well?"

Natasha helped herself to a dainty morsel of fish. "Indeed. And you?"

Ishbu interrupted. "Tash, tell Freddy how you got here. He hasn't heard your story yet." He scratched his ear with his hind paw.

Frederick stopped eating. So Natasha was the third survivor?

"Yes," he said. "Tell me, Tash." He suddenly felt bold and playful.

Natasha put down her fish and licked her paws. "I am sailing my yacht from Buenos Aires to Rangoon. The race for the Rattigan Cup, you know it? It is very famous. I lose two years in a row and am determined not to lose again this year.

"But tragedy strikes, and I am blown off course. The yacht, she capsizes. I am champion swimmer. But even I cannot swim through ocean forever! At last I am being rescued by fisher-rats who canoe between these islands. They bring me to this place and, thanks to Dhavala, I am recovering."

Natasha smiled, and Frederick swallowed hard. "You are amazing," he said. "I—I mean, how lucky for all of us the temple was here."

"Not luck." Dhavala had come into the room so silently that Frederick had not heard her. "All things happen for a reason." She held out her paw. "Come. There is something I need you to do for me."

To Frederick's astonishment, she was pointing right at him!

THE TREASURE OF KARNI MATA

FREDERICK STARED AT DHAVALA, who nodded and gestured for him to follow.

He trailed after her into the courtyard. Tonight there were no lanterns or torches. Only a few small oil lamps flickered in the dark, which were all the rats needed.

Dhavala directed him to one of the rat holes at the base of the wall. She crawled inside. Frederick's heart tripped eagerly. He'd been longing to explore some of the tunnels!

"Come!" called Dhavala.

The tunnel led underground. Frederick smelled the damp, moist earth and the scent of hundreds of rats. The familiar odor reminded him of his family's nest in the pet shop.

The tunnel seemed to run for miles. Frederick's whiskers brushed the dirt on either side, indicating that the passage was narrow.

Frederick heard Dhavala scrabble upward, and soon he too was scrambling up. He popped out of the hole and was surprised to find himself in a small room. Here he smelled earth, rats, and something musty and mysterious. It smelled like time—time past and ancient.

Dhavala stood close to Frederick, her breath on his cheek, her voice hushed. "Before I light the lantern, let me explain: In the main temple of Karni Mata, if a man killed or injured a rat, he would donate a rat figure made of gold or silver as atonement. Over the centuries our temple became filled with these figures. When my ancestors came here, they brought some of them, including one that was most special."

A draft ruffled Frederick's fur. Or was it fear?

Dhavala continued her tale: "For centuries we have hidden our greatest treasure in this temple. Only the high priestess is allowed to see it, to clean and polish it. This I have done for many years."

Now Dhavala's voice dropped so low that Frederick could hardly make out the words. He leaned in closer, so close their whiskers brushed. A sudden dread chilled him to his marrow.

"Three weeks ago, as I polished the treasure, I noticed an inscription that had not been there before. I told no one but immediately moved the statue. I wished to ponder upon this mystery alone." She paused and curled her long tail around her paws.

"My friend, we are simple rats, content to work, to live in peace, to please our Mother. We have no education. No one in the temple can read this inscription. Not even myself."

She stepped back, her voice trembling with emotion. "Frederick, we have heard much of you from your brother. It is my hope that you might tell us the meaning of these strange symbols.

"Behold," she said. And she lit the lantern.

At once the little room was filled with brilliant flashes of color. The light sparkled off emeralds, rubies, diamonds, and gold. Frederick's eyes grew big as he gazed upon the treasure of Karni Mata.

Gleaming in the lantern light was a statue so magnificent that Frederick knew without being told that this was the fabled Burmese Bandicoot!

THE MYSTERIOUS
INSCRIPTION

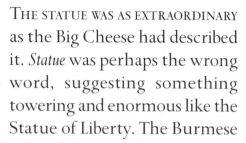

THE STATUE WAS AS EXTRAORDINARY as the Big Cheese had described it. *Statue* was perhaps the wrong word, suggesting something towering and enormous like the Statue of Liberty. The Burmese Bandicoot was small, about the size of a young rat, more like a figurine, really. But still astonishing.

Unlike its rodent namesake, the Burmese Bandicoot was completely covered with gems. Sparkles of red, green, and white glittered like fireworks. Frederick had never seen anything so wondrous. He recalled the Big Cheese telling him how originally it had been made to please a beautiful woman. No wonder she had liked it!

Frederick turned to look at Dhavala, standing tall and regal, her front paws folded over her chest and her eyes half closed, as if listening to music only she could hear.

Dhavala opened her eyes and shook herself all over. "The inscription," she murmured. "I must show you the inscription."

She took Frederick by the paw and led him close to the statue. Bending down, she pointed to the base. Frederick saw a series of strange marks in the gold.

"Is it a message from the Mother? Can you tell me what it says?" Dhavala sounded more unsure than Frederick had ever heard her.

He bent low and strained to see the marks. They were crudely etched into the gold at the base— shallow and poorly made. It didn't look like a divine inscription but rather like something a child might scratch out for fun. He leaned closer.

Now he could see that the marks were letters and numerals. But they meant nothing to him. He read them aloud, repeating them to himself. It wasn't English. And it didn't look like Spanish or French or German or the Asian characters he'd seen in books. But somehow it did look familiar . . . like something he'd seen in class. . . .

37°46'30" N   122°25'10" W

He slapped a paw to his forehead. "Coordinates!" he cried. "From Miss Dove's geography lesson!"

Dhavala took a step forward. "You can translate it then?" she asked eagerly.

"They're latitude and longitude coordinates! It

gives the location of a place." Frederick grinned. "Simple, really. Once you've learned about it."

"But what is the place?" asked Dhavala. "And why is it on the statue?"

Frederick scratched his nose. "I don't know. Without a map I can't tell."

Dhavala looked disappointed. "So it is a human-thing." She sighed. "Not a message to us from the Mother?"

"I don't see how it could be," Frederick said. "I don't think these kind of map coordinates were even used until the seventeen hundreds. It isn't an ancient inscription at all."

Dhavala waved her paw. "Let us go." Her voice sounded sad. She extinguished the lantern. Frederick was sorry to leave the captivating figurine behind.

Dhavala led the way back down the tunnel to the courtyard. At the tunnel's entrance, she turned to Frederick.

"One mystery yet remains," she said, brushing the dust from her whiskers. "Since it is not a miracle, the inscription must have been written on the treasure by someone here. In the temple. But who? And why?"

"MY ONLY HOPE"

DHAVALA LEFT FREDERICK IN THE courtyard, saying she had many matters to attend to before dawn. He watched her walk away, her body bent by time and worry. He regretted that he hadn't been able to help her. She was gone before he realized that he hadn't told her how he'd heard of this treasure before.

Natasha and Ishbu scampered up. They had obviously been waiting for him and nearly danced in anticipation.

"Well?" asked Ishbu. "Tell us! What did Dhavala want? Where did she take you?"

Frederick combed the dust from his fur as he described what he'd seen.

Ishbu's eyes widened. He tugged Frederick's tail. "Freddy, isn't that the—"

Frederick put his paw over Ishbu's mouth and

looked around to make sure they were not over-heard. "That's right, Ishbu," he said quietly. "The Burmese Bandicoot!" Beside him Natasha let out her breath in a long, slow sigh.

Frederick turned to look at her. She gazed off into the distance, her lips slightly parted. Her elegant nose twitched as if she smelled something delicious. Frederick wondered if the beautiful woman for whom the Burmese Bandicoot had been made was as lovely as Natasha.

Disturbed, Ishbu sat down on the courtyard floor and began to wash his paws and whiskers. The other two followed suit.

Frederick nibbled between his toes. "It was mag-nificent," he said in a dreamy voice. "Think of it, Ishbu!"

"Sure. If you say so, Freddy. But there's some-thing mighty strange about the whole setup if you ask me." Ishbu scratched behind his ears. "I can't put my paw on it. Never mind. It will come to me. I'm famished. Let's find some food."

The three rats found their way to the temple kitchens and raided the cupboards, snacking on coconut and pineapple.

When Ishbu went off to get more coconut, Natasha pulled Frederick aside.

"Frederick, you must help me." Her eyelashes fluttered, and so did Frederick's heart.

Frederick stopped eating, a morsel of pineapple halfway to his mouth. The cinnamon scent of Natasha's fur made his head spin. He nodded.

"Dhavala tells to you the lie. This figure does not belong to the temple! It belongs to me." Her voice broke. "Made for my ancestress by a maharajah long ago. My family has been owning her for generations. She was never given to the temple! Never!"

Her eyes sparkled with tears. "Sadly, many years ago, she was stolen from me. I have been searching for her all this time. Now, thanks to you, I have found her! You must get her back for me." She looked at Frederick, pleading. "You are my only hope." She put one delicate paw on his foreleg.

Frederick thrilled beneath her touch. He had always seen himself as a hero, fighting dragons, exploring new lands, rescuing princesses—and now here was his opportunity to save a damsel in distress!

Ishbu returned with the coconut, and Natasha put her paw to her lips, warning Frederick to say nothing. Ishbu chattered away as they finished their snack, never noticing the silence of the other two.

It was dawn when the rats parted. Natasha said good day first, standing on her toes to brush Frederick's whiskers lightly with her own. "Bring it to my burrow today," she murmured. "I know I can count on you."

Frederick blushed down to the tip of his tail.

Ishbu watched, his paws folded against his chest, as Natasha glided down the passageway to her chamber.

"There's something fishy about that rat, Freddy," he said. "Watch out for her."

"Who?" asked Frederick, still dreaming of Natasha's cinnamon fragrance, her shiny black eyes, and her charming accent. "Dhavala? I'm starting to like her."

Ishbu snorted. "Not Dhavala. Mark my words, Freddy. There's something strange going on."

A THIEF IN BROAD DAYLIGHT

FREDERICK COULDN'T SLEEP. Sunlight streamed into the little chamber. Night was long past, and most of the temple rats were sleeping. His nest of soft fur and feathers seemed scratchy and hard. He tossed and turned and finally got up.

What he was about to do was the right thing, he was sure of it. Absolutely sure . . . It wasn't theft. The statue belonged to Natasha. It was her property in the first place, and he was just giving it back to her. Returning stolen property! That's what it was! It was the right—the *honest*—thing to do.

He groomed quickly, thinking of Natasha. How she would gaze at him when he brought her the Burmese Bandicoot! She would flutter her eyelashes. Maybe she would brush his whiskers with hers again. He sighed. He would be a true hero! Natasha's hero!

He deliberately squashed the picture of Dhavala from his mind. The statue didn't belong to her; in fact, it didn't belong in the temple at all, hidden away in the dark and the dirt, where no one could appreciate it. No, it belonged with Natasha. Anyone would agree. Anyone!

Even Ishbu would understand.

But just in case he didn't, Frederick didn't tell his brother where he was going.

He sneaked out in the full glare of daylight, squinting against the sun. The courtyard was deserted. Faint snores came from the burrows and chambers all around. Sniffing hard, Frederick found the right tunnel, and he raced straight to the end. His heart slammed against his ribs. Not because he was doing anything wrong. Just because he was running. Yes, that was it! He was just exercising. Anyone's heart would pound. Anyone's!

He lit the match he'd taken from the kitchen. In the flare of light the gems flickered like fireflies. Frederick's breath caught in his throat upon seeing the statue again. It was just as glorious as he remembered.

But he couldn't stand here all day admiring it. Natasha waited. He grabbed the Burmese Bandicoot and stuffed it in the burlap sack he'd brought. He glanced around quickly. He was alone. No one saw. So why did he have this feeling of being watched?

He shook himself all over to get rid of the feeling. Then he dashed back down the narrow tunnel. He carried the sack with the statue in his teeth, supporting the weight of it on his back. Now to find Natasha.

∞

Many hours later, when the moon had risen and all of the temple rats were awake and going about their business, Frederick sat at the table in the great hall. Ishbu sat next to him, nibbling on cashews and tuna; but it was late and the hall was nearly empty. Frederick yawned, stretching out his pink tongue. He hadn't had much sleep all day, but his whiskers curled with pleasure as he remembered Natasha thanking him. . . .

A scrawny old fisher-rat, smelling strongly of sardines and saltwater, entered the chamber, bowed to Frederick, and handed him a note. Surprised, Frederick took it. There was nothing written on the outside. Ishbu told the fisher-rat to help himself to some food, and the messenger sat down next to them.

Frederick unfolded the note.

My darling Frederick,
Please think well of me while
you are battling sharks and I
am basking on the Riviera. You

*are just the kind of rat I like—
strong, brave, and stupid. Don't
try to find me—your life would
be in danger.
     Love and kisses,
     Natasha*

Frederick read it again and again. The first time, he couldn't believe it. The second time, his heart broke. He could hear it shatter.

Ishbu saw Frederick's ears droop and took the note from his limp paw. He read it and then turned to the fisher-rat.

"Where did you get this?" Ishbu demanded, crumpling the note in his paw.

"The girl rat, the pretty one. She paid me to take her to Bangkok. She was in a big hurry."

"Was she alone?"

"Yes. Just the girl. I dropped her at the pier." The fisher-rat helped himself to a big piece of tuna.

"Was she carrying anything?" Frederick asked urgently.

The old rat shook his tattered ears. "Nothing." He chewed slowly with his broken, yellow teeth and swallowed.

Frederick sat back, relieved.

The fisher-rat scratched his nose. "Unless you mean that burlap sack. It looked heavy."

Frederick was thunderstruck. Natasha had played him for a sap! The Burmese Bandicoot wasn't hers! She was a thief! A common thief! He groaned.

Dhavala entered, her fur ruffled. "The treasure! It's gone!" she cried. She looked at Frederick. "What have you done?"

Ishbu jumped up. "He hasn't done anything! It was Natasha. Natasha took the treasure!"

Frederick moaned and shook his ears. "No, Ishbu. Dhavala's right. It's all my fault. I stole the statue and gave it to Natasha."

Ishbu's mouth dropped. He stared at Frederick. "You *stole* it? But why?"

Frederick's shoulders slumped. "Natasha told me it was hers."

"And you believed her?" Ishbu glared. "I can't believe you fell for that. I told you she was up to something. Freddy! How could you?"

Frederick put his head in his paws and groaned again. Ishbu was right. He was a chump. A sucker. A dope. A fool. Not a hero at all.

Dhavala interrupted. "It's much worse than you realize." She slid into the space next to them and signaled the fisher-rat to leave. He bowed and left the chamber at once.

Dhavala's voice dropped to a whisper: "The Burmese Bandicoot wasn't merely our treasure. There was a reason we took it from India all those centuries ago. It was our duty to guard and protect it."

She paused, her gentle face creased with worry. "The statue conceals a secret so deadly that it could wipe humankind from the face of the earth."

BETRAYAL

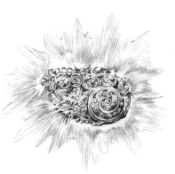

Ishbu gasped. "Wipe out humans! What do you mean?"

Dhavala rubbed her paws anxiously. "Only the high priestess of the temple has this knowledge, passed down for generations." She paced across the marble floor. "I would not be telling you now if I did not need your help most desperately." Her wrinkled face looked even older than usual.

Frederick's heart slid into his tail. It was all his fault. If only he hadn't fallen for Natasha's charms!

Dhavala looked at them both, her eyes wet. "The statue is hollow," she told them. "Inside is a compartment containing a packet of ancient herbs. It was the job of the temple rats—and the high priestess above all—to conceal and guard this packet so that it wouldn't fall into the wrong hands. And now it is gone!"

Ishbu leaped up. "That's awful!" he exclaimed. He sat back down and started grooming. "Wait, I don't get it. What's the big deal about a little packet of herbs?"

Dhavala stopped pacing. "Poison," she said; and although she spoke softly, the word seemed to echo through the hall. "These herbs are the only known mixture of an ancient poison. One that works on humans but not on animals."

"Like rat poison in reverse," muttered Ishbu. He looked over at Frederick, who still sat slumped and dejected. He wouldn't meet their eyes.

"It was concocted centuries ago to give animals a defense against humans should they ever need one," continued Dhavala. "It is said to be untraceable and undetectable. Dropped into a large body of drinking water—a reservoir or lake—it could exterminate all of the humans who drink from this source!"

"But the statue couldn't contain enough to poison all humans," said Ishbu. "There must be billions of them. They are everywhere."

"It is so deadly that only a drop is needed," said Dhavala. "If there was a way to contaminate enough water supplies, humankind would perish, leaving Earth to the animals."

The three rats sat in silence for some time. Ishbu chewed his toenails again. Dhavala rubbed her paws. And Frederick, poor Frederick sat in misery, having heard only half of the conversation, still nursing a guilty, broken heart.

"Frederick," urged Dhavala. "We need your help, your intelligence, your education. What can we do to stop this?"

Frederick perked up a little. Perhaps he could redeem himself. "Not enough poison in the statue to exterminate all humans. . . ." He paused. "But a laboratory could analyze the formula and make more."

"But what kind of animal could do such a truly wicked thing?" asked Dhavala.

"Natasha stole the statue. But maybe she didn't know about the poison. Maybe she just wanted it for the jewels," said Frederick hopefully.

Ishbu shook his ears. "I think she *did* know. I suspected she was up to no good. She was always nosing around the temple. Listen! What if she found the Burmese Bandicoot when she first got here?"

"Then why not just take it? Why convince me to steal it for her?" Frederick winced as he remembered how gullible he'd been.

"Maybe she was waiting for someone else. An accomplice," suggested Ishbu.

"And remember, I moved the statue," Dhavala reminded them. "She hadn't known where it was hidden during the last two weeks. You were the only one I told, Frederick, because I hoped you could decode the inscription."

"The inscription!" shouted Frederick, leaping to his paws. "Maybe *she* wrote it!"

"But why? What does the inscription mean?" asked Dhavala.

"We know it is map coordinates," said Frederick, "giving the location of a place." He thought hard, nibbling the end of his tail. "So it might have told someone where to take the statue. . . ."

"Delivery instructions!" cried Ishbu, brandishing a banana. "Listen, Freddy! Natasha gets to the island and pretends she's a shipwreck victim. She finds the statue and marks it with the place to deliver it. She waits for—"

"The captain of the *General Custer* to arrive!" Frederick shouted again. "It fits! It fits!" He turned to Ishbu, his eyes blazing. "Remember how we overheard the captain say he was supposed to pick up the statue for someone? Remember how Natasha wanted to know if the captain or crew survived the wreck?"

He spun around. "How about this: Natasha steals the statue. She'll take it to a drop point. The captain will pick it up; his map shows the place. The inscription on the statue—the coordinates—tells him where to deliver the statue and pick up his payment. Natasha plans to escape the island on her own later."

Frederick's words came faster and faster. "What an ingenious scheme! No humans ever see any animals directly."

"But the *Custer* sinks." Ishbu picked up the tale and a piece of mango. "The captain never collects the statue. Natasha figures she'll have to deliver it herself."

"Except by then I have seen the inscription and hidden the statue," added Dhavala, "and Natasha can't find it. She must have been terribly frustrated."

Frederick sat down suddenly, as deflated as a balloon. "And then I show up," he said sadly. "Like a sap, like a fall guy, like the answer to her prayer. Ready to be taken in and take the blame."

Ishbu nipped him gently on the shoulder to cheer him up.

"There's still one thing we must know," said Dhavala. She picked up a palm frond and rolled it between her paws. "Where is Natasha taking the statue? She must be stopped."

Frederick nibbled his toenails pensively. He had to figure out the location of those coordinates!

SECRET CODES
AND CIPHERS

IF FREDERICK HAD A MAP, A CHART, or a globe, he would have been able to look up the lines of longitude and latitude and see where they crossed. That would give him the correct location. Alas, he didn't have any of these. A GPS (global positioning device) would have been helpful too, but he didn't have one of those either.

But he did have courage, strength, a good memory, and a fine education. Would that be enough?

He stopped chewing his toenails and concentrated on the problem. "I memorized the coordinates. Latitude: thirty-seven degrees, forty-six minutes, thirty seconds North. Longitude: one hundred twenty-two degrees, twenty-five minutes, ten seconds West. But where is that?"

Ishbu licked mango juice from his paws and leaned closer. "'Fraid I can't help you, Freddy. I guess I napped through that part of class."

Frederick ignored him. He recalled Miss Dove's explanation of latitude: *Remember,* lat *means* fat, *and you'll always know that latitude goes around.*

"Lines of latitude tell how far above or below the equator a place is," he told Dhavala and Ishbu. Frederick was lecturing now, like Miss Dove. All his depression had evaporated. He was in his element— using his knowledge to find a solution!

"Hmm." He scratched behind his ear. "Thirty-seven degrees North. Above the equator. So it's in the Northern Hemisphere.

"The next set of numbers gives longitude," he continued. *Lines of longitude go up and down Earth, like the segments of a peeled orange.*

"Those numbers tell us how far we are from the prime meridian—the line of longitude that passes through Greenwich, England," explained Frederick. "One hundred twenty-two degrees West. So this place is west of England. A long ways west—more than a third of the way around the world actually, since there are three hundred and sixty degrees in a circle around the earth." He stroked his whiskers.

Ishbu raised his paw.

Frederick ignored him again and went on. "If I remember right, the forty-fifth parallel (or line of latitude) passes through Salem, Oregon, at about one hundred twenty-three degrees longitude. That means the location is south of Oregon." He wasn't a teacher—he was a detective!

"The Big Cheese," said Ishbu quietly. "Don't forget the Big Cheese."

Frederick didn't respond. "So the coordinates indicate some place south of Salem, but not too far. Eugene, Oregon? Santa Rosa, California? Yes, I believe it must be somewhere in California." He turned mid-pace and smoothed his whiskers.

"The headquarters of the Big Cheese," Ishbu repeated louder.

Frederick pivoted on his hind paw and paced in the other direction, his tail held high. "If I'm not mistaken, the thirty-fourth parallel passes through Los Angeles, so this is someplace north of L. A. and south of Salem—"

"Freddy! Listen to me!" shouted Ishbu, grabbing Frederick's shoulders and shaking him. "It's the headquarters of the Big Cheese! Natasha's taking the Burmese Bandicoot to the Big Cheese!"

Frederick's mouth dropped open. "Of course!" he cried, grabbing Ishbu in a hug. "That's why the coordinates looked so familiar. San Francisco! The Big Cheese! How could I be so blind?" He clicked his teeth at Ishbu. "Brilliant deduction, Ishbu! How did you do it?"

Ishbu blushed modestly. "It just makes sense. The Big Cheese wants the statue. The Big Cheese has his paw in every pie. The Big Cheese hates humans. He's a bad guy, she's a bad girl. Who else would Natasha work for?"

Frederick sat down. "So the Big Cheese hired Natasha to find the statue and the captain to deliver it." He nodded. "It all fits now."

Dhavala set her paws down heavily on the table, making Frederick jump. He'd forgotten she was there. "I have heard of this Big Cheese," she said. "The contents of the Burmese Bandicoot must never fall into his evil paws. You must stop Natasha."

A thought struck Frederick like a lightning bolt. "Ishbu! She's taking the poison to our city! The children! Miss Dove! They're in danger!"

WISHING FOR WINGS

THEY HAD TO GET OFF THE ISLAND and back to San Francisco immediately. They had to stop Natasha from delivering the Burmese Bandicoot to the Big Cheese. Miss Dove's life and the lives of the schoolchildren depended on them!

But how could they do it?

"Is there a ferry to the mainland?" asked Frederick, jumping up.

Dhavala shook her ears.

"A plane? A road? A bridge? There must be something! How do you get food? Supplies?" Frederick demanded, his whiskers bristling.

"No plane, no road," answered Dhavala. "We have no regular trade with the mainland. We grow and forage for all our own food. Anything else we need, the fisher-rats bring when they come."

"How about the fisher-rats then?" asked Ishbu. "Couldn't we travel with them to Bangkok and catch a plane, as Natasha must have?"

Dhavala smoothed her whiskers thoughtfully. "It's possible. But the fisher-rats follow the schools of fish. I do not expect them back for many weeks."

"We can't wait that long!" cried Frederick, pounding his paw on the table. The dishes rattled. "By then who knows what will have happened? We've got to stop Natasha now!" He began to pace again, his long tail dragging behind him.

A breeze wafted through the open archway and set the gold-and-pink silk panels fluttering against the wall. The candles flickered.

"Could you build another sailboat?" said Ishbu.

"It would take weeks to sail to America." Frederick groaned. "Months even. Oh, this is all my fault. If only I hadn't fallen for her lies." His heart squeezed painfully as he remembered her cinnamon fragrance and her whiskers brushing against his.

Ishbu picked up another piece of mango. "If only we had a really fast boat, like a speedboat or a submarine. . . ." He stopped, his mouth full.

"If only, if only," snapped Frederick. "If only we had wings we could fly! We've got to get off this island!"

But how? It's impossible! There was absolutely no

way. Zero, naught, none, nil.

"She has too much of a head start," said Ishbu sadly, licking the mango juice off his paws. "We'll never catch her."

Frederick was staring at the silk fluttering in the breeze—as light as a butterfly's wings. "Wings," he murmured, "if only we had wings."

He darted over and jerked a silk panel from the wall. Ishbu stopped grooming and stared at his brother as if he'd gone crazy.

Maybe he had. Frederick was laughing, laughing and spinning around and around, holding the length of gold-and-pink silk, letting it float behind him—like a veil, like a kite—as light as air. "Look! Look! Don't you see?" he called.

He stopped spinning and held out the silk. "We don't need wings to fly!"

THE AEROSTAT

 ISHBU STARED. "WHAT DO YOU mean?"

"We'll build an aerostat!" said Frederick. "A craft that is lighter than air!"

Ishbu shook his ears while Frederick shook the silk panel. "Don't you get it, Ishbu? We'll make a hot-air balloon!"

Ishbu's ears shot up. "A hot-air balloon? Freddy, have you gone mad? Has the hot tropical sun melted your brain?"

Frederick raced over, the length of silk billowing behind him. "No, no! I'm completely sane. Look. It will work. Watch!"

Frederick leaped onto the low table. Rolling the silk into a cylinder, he held it for a moment over the candle, careful to keep it far enough above the flame so it wouldn't catch fire. The cylinder of silk filled with air heated by the candle's flame and bellied out, like a sail in the wind. Dhavala looked puzzled, but Ishbu's whiskers bristled. "I get it!" he cried, leaping to his paws.

"We'll stitch it together like a balloon," Frederick said, bringing down the silk and folding it up. "Like a bag. We can weave a basket out of palm fronds and attach it with thread. The basket will be our gondola. We'll ride in it."

"But Freddy, will it hold us?" Ishbu asked nervously.

"I believe it will." Frederick dipped his paw in the mango juice and wrote on a linen napkin. "Let's see. I weigh about eight ounces and you weigh, what? Ten, eleven?"

Ishbu blushed. He'd eaten well at the temple. "Better make it twelve ounces, just to be on the safe side."

Frederick spit on his paw and erased some figures, muttered, scratched his ears, and wrote some more—rapidly calculating the weight of the two rats and the proposed basket and the lift needed to get them airborne. Finally he looked up. "I've got it!"

Even though Miss Dove hadn't covered astroengineering, aerostatic design, or advanced calculus in her fifth-grade class, Frederick—like Albert Einstein, Marie Curie, Sir Isaac Newton, and Leonardo da Vinci—was able to take what he'd learned, add a flash of inspiration, a smidgeon of genius, and a little bit of luck, and create something new.

"But what will we do for fuel?" asked Ishbu. "A hot-air balloon needs hot air, right?"

Frederick rubbed his nose and thought back to last fall. The fifth graders had built balloons out of plastic bags and fueled them with hair dryers. What a pity there was no electricity on the island! And no electrical cord long enough to reach from here to the nearest outlet!

"We'll have to use candles," Frederick told Ishbu. He wondered how many candles they would need. He erased some more figures. He'd have to recalculate to allow for the weight of the candles.

"My friends." Dhavala's soft voice interrupted. "I believe I understand this contraption you speak of. I have heard stories of the fire balloons of Myanmar and northern Laos. In the eighth month, on the night of the full moon, humans make paper balloons in the shapes of roosters, elephants, and cows. Into each they place a tiny oil lamp that fills the paper with hot air. The fire balloons rise, glowing in the dark like lanterns, welcoming Buddha back from Heaven."

"That's it!" cried Frederick, his eyes shining. "We'll use oil lamps. They'll weigh less and burn longer!"

He made a few more notations and then rolled up the napkin with his carefully calculated figures. "Done. Let's get some sleep. It's nearly dawn. Tonight we'll build the balloon."

"And fly to America," said Ishbu.

"And rescue Miss Dove," said Frederick.

"And save the world," added Dhavala.

"BY THE DAWN'S EARLY LIGHT"

THROUGH THE HEROIC EFFORT OF every rat in the temple, the balloon was constructed in a single night. Dhavala's priestesses, who were skilled seamstresses as well, quickly cut and stitched the silk panels into a balloon according to Frederick's pattern. Weaving the palm frond basket was rapidly accomplished, as was sewing the basket—or gondola as Frederick called it—to the balloon.

The rats worked all night; and by dawn the next day, the balloon was finished.

It was an incredible sight! The silk balloon was anchored on the beach, away from the mangrove trees, so it would be easy to launch. Tethered to the ground with twine, it bobbed in the light, tropical breeze like a huge, pink-and-gold beach ball. Beneath the silk balloon, the gondola looked tiny and frail. *But so had my barrel*, thought Frederick, *and it did the trick.*

The temple rats gathered around in the early morning sunlight. Dhavala, Ishbu, and Frederick stood a little apart from the crowd, looking at their idea come to life. Frederick shivered. It was a sight to tell his children and grandchildren about for generations to come.

Ishbu caught his breath. "Are you sure it's safe?" he asked, his teeth chattering.

"As sure as I can be," said Frederick. "I've run the calculations a hundred times."

Dhavala handed Frederick a jug of coconut milk.

"I christen this balloon the *Amelia Earhart!*" Frederick shouted, tapping the jug against the basket. Coconut milk spilled across the sand. The temple rats cheered.

"Look here," he said to Ishbu, "I have our itinerary all planned out." Frederick unrolled a sheet of paper on which he had drawn a crude map.

"We have no motor, so we can't steer or speed up or slow down," Frederick explained, pointing to his chart. "But by increasing or decreasing the amount of fuel we burn, we can raise and lower the balloon. At different altitudes, we can catch different winds. Like hitching a ride!

"By heading west," he continued, "we'll have opportunities to land and refuel." He paused and rubbed his nose thoughtfully. "As long as we don't get caught in a storm."

Ishbu peered at the map. He had no idea what it all meant, but if Freddy said so, he believed it. He rolled up the map and handed it back to Frederick. "I'm sure you're right. But what about meals?"

Dhavala stepped forward with a small rattan basket. "We have prepared some food for your journey." Her brown eyes shone gratefully. "You will accomplish your task. I feel it. The blessings of Karni Mata go with you."

Ishbu and Frederick thanked her. They lightly brushed whiskers with Dhavala and clicked their teeth good-bye to all the temple rats. (Ishbu's teeth were chattering more from nerves than farewells.)

Ishbu clutched the basket of food. Frederick climbed into the gondola first, and then Ishbu handed him the basket and scrambled up, using his tail for balance. He slipped, and Frederick caught him under his arms and hauled him in headfirst, his little hind paws scrabbling for footholds.

Once on board, Frederick untied the twine tethering them to the earth. He opened the burner wider, and—freed from its leash—the balloon rose slowly into the sky.

They were on their way!

Part Three: SKY

In gallant trim the gilded vessel goes . . .
—Thomas Gray

UP, UP, AND AWAY

Two rats riding in a hot-air balloon across India, the Middle East, Europe, and the Atlantic Ocean seems incredible—but that's exactly what Frederick and Ishbu planned to do.

The balloon floated up above the island. The crowd of rats below looked as tiny as peas. Frederick was entranced by the sight of the white sand beach and green jungle growing smaller and smaller as they flew. Ishbu was airsick (which felt a lot like being seasick, oddly enough).

The uncharted island of the Secret Temple of Karni Mata shrank to a sandy blob. The coral reef, the breakers, the sea—all appeared flat and serene, and postcard pretty. The waves looked like satin and the palm trees like the cardboard cutouts in the dioramas made by Miss Dove's fifth graders.

All morning they sailed over the Indian Ocean.

The air was warm and pleasant. A steady breeze blew them toward India, their first destination.

On such a beautiful day, on such an amazing ride, it was hard to believe that there was wickedness in the world. The plans of a criminal mastermind, the toxic threat to humankind—both seemed too absurd to be true. But then so did the idea of two rats in a flying balloon. . . . Like the Burmese Bandicoot, this beautiful day hid evil within.

To avoid his worrisome thoughts, Frederick made notes on air currents, speed, lift, and the amount of oil they had burned already. Ishbu nibbled on their snacks and napped in the shade of the balloon.

The breeze buoyed them up and up. The balloon swam in an ocean of air that deepened to cobalt blue above and below. A bouquet of white clouds bloomed on the horizon.

It was like the first day of summer vacation, when Miss Dove always took the rats home: time slowed down. The warm sun beat upon their fur and sparkled like silver on the waves far beneath them. The air smelled of seaweed and tropical flowers. Frederick's pen slowed and then stopped altogether as, lulled by the warmth and exhausted from staying up the day before, he fell into a deep sleep.

He dreamed he was back at W. H. E. S. The red brick walls. Miss Dove's classroom. The old linoleum floors echoing with footsteps. The dry smell of chalk dust. Millicent Mallory and Kay Serah were there, hiding in the corner by Miss Dove's desk. Then they were gone, and Natasha was there instead, batting her silky eyelashes. She was going to bite Miss Dove on the hand. Frederick growled. "Stop!" he cried.

The sky grew dark as clouds scudded across the sun. Frederick shivered but didn't wake. It was only a dream. Or was it?

Natasha and Miss Dove vanished. The Big Cheese appeared, his milky blind eyes as opaque as opals. He carried the Burmese Bandicoot in the crook of his elbow. The jewels flashed red, green, and gold. Suddenly the opossum turned into Igor, the Nightmare King, his massive coils towering over Frederick.

Frederick whimpered but still didn't wake. He grabbed the world globe that appeared in his paw and threw it, striking the snake. It burst like a balloon, drenching them both in glitter. Then everyone disappeared except Miss Dove, who now sat at her desk, holding Frederick in her hand and stroking his fur. He was a hero!

A violent gust of cold wind woke him. The silk of the balloon cracked like a whip.

"Ishbu! Wake up! Help me!" yelled Frederick, desperately grabbing hold of the line. The gondola snapped back and forth, tipping dangerously. The sky was dark. The wind roared around them, whistling and howling. Rain poured down.

They had caught the Bengal cyclone.

CATCH A TIGER BY THE TAIL

LIKE ALL SCIENTISTS, FREDERICK knew that even though calculations may be perfect (as his were), the results may not be exactly as expected. The Bengal cyclone was not a slow train across the Indian Ocean upon which any passenger might hitch a ride. The cyclone was a wild wind—a whirling dervish; a soaking, blowing, pouring, howling, roaring, whistling monster of a wind— that streamed and screamed across the Indian Ocean.

It was a shame Miss Dove hadn't spent more time on the local winds of the Indian Ocean, but even the best teacher can't cover everything. If she had covered Bengal cyclones, Frederick would have known this was nothing to mess with. Like a Bengal tiger, it snarled and growled, tugged and tore, picking up water and speed until it blasted onshore. It led the way for the infamous Indian monsoons, the drenching rainstorms that flood Asia every year. Had Frederick been sailing over the Pacific Ocean, it would have been called a hurricane.

Frederick heard the fragile silk of the balloon rip. He needed duct tape! But it would have been too late. When the wind snuffed out the oil flame, the balloon deflated. The basket swung crazily from side to side in the dark and rainy sky, nearly tipping out Frederick and Ishbu. Frederick's careful charts flew overboard, scattering like a flock of frightened doves. The food followed. Ishbu grabbed for it and would have fallen out had Frederick not seized him by the tail and dragged him back in.

The balloon plunged toward the ocean. Frederick saw that the water, so blue and tranquil before, was now as gray as steel and studded with whitecaps that looked as hard as concrete. Down they whirled, faster and faster. Plummeting, plunging, they fell toward the sea like an elevator in free fall.

Ishbu's tummy dropped. His ears and whiskers streamed back. He closed his eyes and clutched Frederick. Frederick held on to Ishbu and wrapped his tail around the cord. If he could hold on, maybe the silk would act as a parachute.

And maybe that would have worked—if the day had stayed fine, warm, mild, sunny. There are stories of deflated hot-air balloons opening like parachutes and drifting gently back to Earth. But not this one. Not in a raging Bengal cyclone. Not for these two brave rats.

The rain soaked the silk and the wind shredded it. Now the heavy, wet silk dragged the basket down, an anchor pulling them to their doom. They fell and fell. The water was so close, they could feel the spray.

Frederick closed his eyes and took a final breath. "Farewell, dear brother . . . ," he gasped, choking out a few last words, when suddenly—

"Hooroo! Hooroo!" Above the noise of the wild wind came another sound, as loud and coarse as a raven's caw.

"Hooroo! Hooroo!"

Frederick opened his eyes. A huge black-and-white bird, bigger than a seagull, flew through the storm, racing the basket in its plunge to the sea. Just before they hit the water, the bird snatched the twine and ripped the basket free from the ruined balloon. The creature spread his powerful wings and carried the basket up above the restless reach of the surf, snatching the brothers from an eternity in Davy Jones's locker.

ALBATROSS ISLAND

CAN A BIRD, EVEN A BIG BIRD, survive a Bengal cyclone? Perhaps not, under ordinary circumstances. But this bird seemed to know exactly what he was doing. He raced in front of the storm, keeping his long wings spread, dipping and swooping with mad glee as the wind drove him along.

Bengal cyclones have been clocked at more than 117 kilometers an hour. The bird should have been terrified, drenched, and miserable, and fighting for his life, his feathers torn and battered. Instead he glided carelessly along the storm track like a kid on a skateboard. Every now and then the rats heard his wild call, "Hooroo! Hooroo!"

Frederick *was* terrified but for Ishbu's sake tried not to show it. He clung to the basket with white-knuckled paws and peered over the side. The wind dashed salt spray in his face, and he shook it off. The bird skimmed the surging waves and then whooshed into the air so high that the ocean looked like a rumpled gray blanket.

Ishbu huddled in the bottom of the basket, sick and green. Rainwater streamed from his ears and whiskers. Frederick dropped down and curled next to his shivering brother. When would it stop? Where would it all end? He expected them to be tossed into the sea at any minute.

Then the basket stopped moving, the wind ceased as if someone had hit the power switch, and everything went dark.

Frederick gingerly climbed to the rim of the basket. It was clear that they had landed, but where? He couldn't see a thing! He smelled the saltwater-fish smell, so he knew they were still somewhere near the ocean. And he heard a distant hollow roar—the wind? The surf? He rubbed his eyes.

Ishbu climbed up beside him. "Freddy!" he whispered. "W-why are we inside a cave?"

That was it. A cave! That was why the wind and rain had stopped so suddenly! That's why it was so dark! As his eyes adjusted to the light from the mouth of the cave, Frederick saw a flock of birds sheltering from the storm. Their heads were tucked under their wings. From time to time he heard a rustling of feathers and a coo as gentle as a sigh.

"G'day, mates," squawked a voice beside them. "Welcome to Albatross Island!"

"W-where?" Ishbu's teeth still chattered.

"Off the coast of Tasmania." The enormous bird preened his black and white feathers as he spoke.

"That's impossible," said Frederick flatly. "We were headed north. To India. Tasmania is miles and miles in the other direction. We can't have got that far south."

"Blown off course, mates," said the bird. "Blown or flown, all the same. Happens all the time in a storm."

Frederick closed his eyes. All his careful charts! All his calculations! Blown off course! Lost in the Southern Ocean! They'd never get back to school in time!

Ishbu, meanwhile, was sniffing the bird. "Say, don't I know you from somewhere?" he asked.

"Right-o, mate! I was wondering when you'd recognize me! I'm Louie! Louie, the albatross!"

"Louie!" cried Ishbu. "Am I ever glad to see you!"

Frederick shook his ears. Who was Louie? And how did Ishbu know him?

"Let me introduce you to my brother!" said Ishbu. He elbowed Frederick in the ribs. "Freddy, this is the albatross I told you about. The one who brought me to the island."

The albatross fluffed up his feathers and bobbed his head.

"Happy to do it, mate. You saved my life, freeing me from that fishing net."

Ishbu shrugged. "I just thought you looked uncomfortable."

"When I saw you dropping from the sky, I says to myself, 'Crikey, there's that little rat again. He done you a good deed, and now it's your turn.' So I scoops up your basket, and here you are."

"Thanks!" said Ishbu. "I thought for sure we were goners that time."

"Yes, thank you very much," added Frederick. "But what were you doing out in the storm?"

The albatross stroked his feathers with his beak. "Me? I'm in training!"

"Training?" the brothers echoed.

"Sure, mates! I'm an athlete! Ever hear of the Australian Big Bird Race?"

They shook their ears.

"From Tasmania to South Africa—ninety-six hundred kilometers. Lose every time, I do. But this is my lucky year, mates. I feel it!"

"You were training for a race in a storm?" Frederick couldn't believe any animal could be so crazy.

The albatross nodded. Bits of feather fluttered down. Ishbu sneezed. "The Bengal cyclone makes the best training ever. Just look at these!" He stretched his vast wings. Tip to tip they almost spanned the cave. "Impresses the ladies too." He winked.

One of the other birds woke up. "Give it a rest, Louie," she muttered, tucking her head beneath her wing. "Some of us want to sleep."

Louie folded his wings back up and lowered his squawk. "I'm in the best shape of my career. I'm a shoe-in to win this year. But now, the real question is, what were two little rats like yourselves doing out in a basket in a Bengal cyclone?"

Frederick quietly summed up all of their adventures—from escaping Mr. Stern's office to the ill-fated flight of the *Amelia Earhart*. Ishbu, who had heard it all before, took the opportunity to doze off, waking only when he heard Frederick say: "And that's why we have to reach San Francisco as soon as possible."

"Crikey!" Louie said. "Saving the world! Good on ya! But sorry to tell you, mate, you're going about it all wrong."

"What!" Frederick exclaimed.

There was a rustling as the other birds in the cave shifted positions.

Frederick lowered his voice. "All wrong? Why?"

"You'd never get there in time flying west. You've got to head south and catch the Roaring Forties."

"What're the Roaring Forties?" asked Ishbu, who had found a barnacle on the floor of the cave and was sucking out the juice.

"The winds at the fortieth parallel," Frederick explained. "Also known as the prevailing westerlies. But Louie! Don't they blow east? Won't that take longer?"

"Not at all. I do it often. Catch a ride on the Roaring Forties to the Pacific Ocean and up the coast on the *cordonazo de San Francisco*."

"'The lash of St. Francis,'" Frederick said, before Ishbu could ask. "I've heard of it. A wind that blows like the crack of a whip, whistling up the coast of Mexico to California." He looked up at Louie. "But would it be safe?"

"Sure," said Louie. "It's in the bag. That is, if you're in shape like me. Buzz up to 'Frisco for tea on the Farallon Islands and then home for spring migration. We'll be there in no time."

Frederick scratched his ears. "You mean you're coming with us?"

The big albatross grinned. "Who else is strong enough to carry the basket, mates?"

THE CITY BY THE BAY

 FLYING TWO RATS IN A BASKET TO San Francisco took longer than Louie thought. Ishbu nervously groomed (when he wasn't sleeping or moaning), while Frederick's worries took over. He chewed his toenails down to the quick as he imagined Natasha handing the Burmese Bandicoot over to the Big Cheese.

At last they were flying over the Golden Gate Bridge. For once the city was not wreathed in fog but lay white and shining on the green hills. Sunset clouds striped the sky in pink and gold. They reminded Frederick of the colors of the *Amelia Earhart*—like the *General Custer*, a doomed name for a doomed craft.

But they were nearly home!

Louie circled the rose-colored dome of the Palace of Fine Arts and splash-landed in the reflecting pond. A regal swan gave him a withering look and sailed off.

"Here you go, mates," he said, paddling over to the bank. "Cable cars, Fisherman's Wharf, Chinatown, Golden Gate Park."

"Home, sweet home," said Ishbu. He scrambled out of the basket and took a long, deep sniff. Sourdough bread. Crab. Chocolate.

Frederick followed. His legs trembled like wet spaghetti after being airborne for so long.

"Well, I'm off. Supper on the Farallon Islands and then back home on the winds. I'll be just in time for the Aussie Big Bird Race. Wish me luck!" Louie squawked, and a nearby flock of sparrows scattered.

"How can we ever repay you?" asked Frederick.

Louie winked. "Just go for it, mates."

"We'll try," said Frederick, hoping it wasn't already too late.

Ishbu ran over to Louie and brushed his whiskers against the big bird's feathers. "Oh, Louie, will you drop us a postcard from Tasmania?"

"Will do!" Louie flapped his wings and took off. "Hooroo! Hooroo!"

The brothers turned to each other and clicked their teeth. It was time to save the world.

ABANDON HOPE,
YE WHO ENTER

THE TWO RATS SCRAMBLED through dark alleys, dirt paths, and twisting back roads to reach the headquarters of the Big Cheese. When they arrived, they crouched behind the garbage bin. The narrow alley lay deep in gloom. The setting sun couldn't penetrate here. Dry leaves blew down the brick-paved street, rattling like bones.

Frederick, followed cautiously by Ishbu, crept around the side of the bin, scoping out the joint. Soon the Bilgewater Brigade would be on patrol, if they weren't already. Frederick shivered, picturing the army of giant rats marching across the warehouse roofs.

A wisp of fog crept up from the wharf. Frederick caught a whiff of garlic, old coffee grounds, and fish guts from the overflowing bin. His stomach growled, and he realized that they hadn't eaten in hours. Even Ishbu was too scared to mention it.

"How will we get in?" whispered Ishbu. "This place must be crawling with guards."

"We need a plan. Let me think." Frederick sat on his haunches and chewed what was left of his toenails. Ishbu found a piece of orange peel and chewed that.

"We can't go through the front," said Frederick. "And we can't go through the back. Too many guards. But there must be a hidden entrance somewhere. Every burrow has one."

While Frederick thought, Ishbu propped himself against a stack of empty cardboard boxes. His tail caught the edge of the stack, and the boxes tipped toward the ground. "Help!" he cried. "They're going to fall."

Frederick dashed over, and together they steadied the tower. Ishbu wiped his brow with his tail in relief. Then the topmost box teetered and fell, hitting the metal bin with a hollow *BANG!* that was as loud as a siren in the empty alley.

"Hey! Who's there?" a rough voice cried out.

Ishbu squeaked in surprise. The brothers turned to run, but two big wharf rats overpowered them and quickly bound them paw and foot. The burly guards stuffed gags in their mouths and blindfolded them. Then they bundled the two hapless, helpless rats off to Headquarters and threw them on the floor somewhere inside. Ishbu landed first, bruising his elbow. Frederick landed on top of him, knocking the breath out of his brother.

"Oof!" said Ishbu.

Frederick heard the door slam shut and the bolt being thrown. Then he heard the *snick-click* of many other locks, one after another. He sniffed the darkness, whiskers trembling.

They were locked in a room in the headquarters of the Big Cheese.

Prisoners.

Who would save the world now?

PRISON BLUES

IF YOU HAVE EVER BEEN CAPTURED by menacing guards—smelling strongly of garlic and mold, their teeth sharp and their paws rough as they rat-handle you and shove you around— well, then, you know how uncomfortable the two rats were. And if you haven't, you must just imagine.

Frederick drew a deep breath through his long, pointed nose. He smelled the musty air of a closet. He smelled Ishbu, the wharf rats, the musk of the ferret, and something else—a hint of cinnamon?

He rolled off Ishbu and tried to sit up. He couldn't move much. He was bound like a mummy, his paws tied behind him with wire and his feet and tail lashed together.

He struggled for several minutes. The wire cut deep into his paws. At last he gave up and lay on the floor, panting. He could hear Ishbu breathing but couldn't see a thing past the blindfold. He couldn't talk around the gag. (This time the guards had not used cotton bandannas.)

He searched through his memory for some iota of information, some drop of data, some kernel of knowledge that might help them escape. He remembered the heroes of the stories Miss Dove had read: What would Robin Hood do? What would King Arthur do? What would Sherlock Holmes or Nancy Drew or Hercules do?

He had an idea. It *might* work. If only Ishbu had been paying attention in class! It was worth a try.

"**A R E Y O U O K** ?" he spelled out in Morse code, clicking his toenail on the wooden floor. (Everyone had loved Miss Dove's lessons on Morse code, learning how to send and receive secret messages.)

"**Y E S**" came the answer. Frederick was amazed! Ishbu had paid attention after all!

"**C A N Y O U E S C A P E** ?" Frederick tapped dots and dashes on the floor and waited for Ishbu's answering clicks.

"**R O L L O V E R H E R E**" came the taps. "**P U T P A W S N E X T T O M I N E . I C A N C U T T H R O U G H** ."

Cut through the wire? Impossible! Still, Frederick inched his way across the floor like a caterpillar across a leaf. He nestled his back against Ishbu's warm, furry shape. Something sawed the wire binding his paws. He grunted as it bit more deeply into his wrists. Then the wire released, and his paws were free!

He sat up and rubbed the circulation back into his paw-tips. When they stopped tingling, he yanked the gag from his mouth and ripped off his blindfold. Light from a crack in the boarded-up window showed him not one, but *two* furry shapes on the floor!

"**H E L P   M E !**" someone tapped.

"Ishbu?" he asked.

"**N O !**" tapped the figure irritably. "**J U S T   G E T   M E   F R E E .**"

He pulled the blindfold and gag from the figure nearest him. He recoiled in surprise. His rescuer wasn't Ishbu.

It was Natasha!

Frederick slapped his brow. Ishbu hadn't remembered Morse code! He'd probably slept through that lesson like all the others. But Natasha, lovely Natasha, the spy for the Big Cheese, of course *she* knew Morse code! She knew latitude and longitude. She probably knew all sorts of things! In spite of himself Frederick felt a twinge of admiration.

"Here," she said. "Use this. I had it concealed when they tied me up." She handed Frederick her nail file.

Perhaps it was foolish of Frederick to release Natasha, but that is exactly what he did. (A brave heart is often a trusting one.) Working quickly, he sawed through the wire binding her forelegs, hind legs, and tail.

Natasha sat up and stretched, while Frederick cut through the wire binding his own hind legs and tail and turned to Ishbu.

He removed Ishbu's blindfold and gag and quickly took care of the wire. Ishbu sat up and rubbed noses with him. Then Ishbu saw Natasha over in the corner, grooming her ears and whiskers. "Freddy! What's she doing here?"

"I was just going to find out," said Frederick.

He looked at Natasha and was moved once again by her beauty: her glossy fur, her silky eyelashes, her elegant white whiskers. He steeled himself against her bewitching charms and said, more harshly than he meant to: "You!"

Natasha ran to him and rubbed whiskers. "You saved me!" she cried. "My hero!" She flung her paws around him.

"Don't trust her, Freddy," said Ishbu. "Remember what happened last time."

Frederick pushed her paws away and stepped back.

"It was big mistake," said Natasha. "Believe me, please. I do not betray you—not you, my brave

Frederick who is saving my life. The evil one, he made me do it. I had no choice!" Her voice broke.

Frederick closed his eyes so he couldn't see her silky eyelashes. He wished he could close his nose so he couldn't smell her cinnamon scent.

She put her paw on his. He was amazed to feel her trembling. "Frederick," she whispered. "Believe me."

Ishbu shook his head. "Don't trust her, Freddy. Listen to *me*."

Frederick looked from one to the other—the beautiful Natasha, his loyal brother. Which one should he believe?

FEMME FATALE?

FREDERICK'S HEAD SWAM. WAS Natasha a victim of circumstances? Or was she working for the Big Cheese? Could Frederick trust her after what she'd done? Could Ishbu forgive him if he did?

Frederick faced Natasha. She held out her paws. He shook his head. He couldn't speak.

Ishbu stepped between them. "If you aren't working for the Big Cheese, what are you doing here?" he asked angrily.

Natasha's eyes filled with tears. "The Big Cheese ratnapped my father! He is telling me he will kill him if I do not do as he says. He forced me to go to the island and find the statue. I am to be marking the statue and hiding it for the captain of the *General Custer*. But everything is going wrong when the ship she sinks. So I think, what can I do? And I know—I will have Frederick bring statue to me, and I will take it to Big Cheese." The more upset she became, the stronger her accent grew.

"Please!" she said. "I am not wanting to hurt you. But I cannot let my father die! What else am I to do?"

She held her paws out to Frederick again. Frederick ignored them. "I am being delayed in Bangkok and only reach Headquarters with the statue yesterday," said Natasha. She picked up her nail file and turned it around and around. She didn't look up.

"I leave a note," she said softly. "I am hoping you will hate me and not try to follow. And that you will be safe." She looked up at him, her eyes shining. "But you do follow! You come for me!" She tried to embrace him, but he backed away.

Ishbu tapped his toenails on the floor. "She still hasn't explained why she's in the headquarters of the Big Cheese." He narrowed his eyes. "I think it's a trap, Freddy. Don't tell her anything!"

Natasha blinked, and a tear rolled down her cheek. "Are you not believing me yet? How am I to be proving myself to you?" She sighed. "It's true I give the statue to the Big Cheese. But I promise you, I am not knowing about the poison! You must believe me!"

She stamped her paw impatiently. "Only tonight

I am learning the Big Cheese has gone somewhere to test this poison. We must stop him!"

"Test?" said Frederick. His ears turned cold. "He's gone? With the poison?"

"Where?" said Ishbu. "Where did the Big Cheese go?"

"I am not remembering." Natasha closed her eyes.

"Try harder!" ordered Frederick. "You must, it's important."

Natasha's eyes flew open. "I am thinking he said a . . . a school!"

ISHBU'S PLAN

"A SCHOOL?" FREDERICK TOOK Natasha by the shoulders. "Which school?" he demanded.

"I think . . . Wilber . . . Force . . . something . . ."

"Wilberforce Harrison Elementary School! I knew it! cried Frederick. "Miss Dove—the children—in danger. Oh, that evil beast!" He gnashed his teeth. "We must get out of here!"

He ran under the boarded-up window and jumped, but the window was too high. He tried scaling the walls, looking for a paw-hold, a toe-hold, any hold, but the walls were too smooth.

"Freddy," said Ishbu. "I think I have a plan."

Frederick stopped and stared at him. Ishbu? A plan?

"I know I'm not an educated rat like you," said Ishbu humbly, "but I think my plan just might work." He turned to Natasha. "We'll need your help."

"You're willing to trust her?" asked Frederick. "After what she did?" He scowled at Natasha.

"I promise," she said. "I am on your side. The Big Cheese locked me up so I could not betray him. That is how you know I tell the truth. If I work for him, would I be a prisoner?"

Ishbu looked at Frederick. "Freddy, we'll have to trust her. It's the only way."

Frederick didn't look convinced, but he nodded slowly. "Just remember," he told her sternly, "I'm keeping my eye on you."

The three rats huddled together, and Ishbu explained his plan.

Frederick gave Natasha a wary look. "Go ahead. It's up to you now."

Natasha handed him her nail file and went to the door. She leaned down and put her snout to the keyhole. "Ooh, rat boys," she cooed. "Yoo-hoo. Are you hungry? I am having some food in here like you would not believe."

"Food?" said a gruff voice. *Ishbu was right*, thought Frederick. *The guards are just outside.*

"Yes, oh my big, strong rat guards," said Natasha. "Big, handsome rat guards will like this food. I have pumpkin pie. I have coconut macaroons. I have sardines!" Natasha winked at Frederick and Ishbu.

"No way," said another rough voice. "There's no

food in there. We'd smell it."

"It couldn't hurt to look," said the first guard. "Maybe she does have food. Pumpkin pie with sardines is my favorite."

"The Big Cheese will kill us if we leave our posts."

"He'll never know. We'll go in, grab the food, and get out. The prisoners are tied up. What could happen? I don't know about you, but I'm starving."

The second guard must have agreed, because the next thing the three rats heard was the key in the lock and the *snick-click* as the bolts were undone. Natasha stepped aside, and the door opened.

Ishbu and Frederick were ready. They jumped the two scruffy rats and knocked them down. Ishbu sat on them while Frederick tied them up with the wire. Natasha grabbed the keys.

The three prisoners raced out, slammed and locked the door, and fled down the corridor to the entrance hole.

Fortunately they didn't encounter any more members of the Bilgewater Brigade, but they knew that it was only a matter of time before their escape was discovered.

Once outside Headquarters Natasha stopped. She brushed Frederick's whiskers, and then Ishbu's, as light as a feather. "For luck," she said.

"You aren't coming?" asked Frederick.

Natasha shook her head. "I go to find my father.

To make sure he is safe. This is your adventure. But perhaps we will meet again someday."

Frederick couldn't help himself—he didn't want her to leave. "May angels speed thee on thy journey," he whispered. He watched her run down the dark alley, the cinnamon scent of her fur already fading.

Ishbu tugged his tail. "Come on, Freddy. Let's go!"

They ran through the alley, racing in and out of the shadows. They sprinted across a bridge to the sound of sirens and the blast of a horn. They crept through backyards beneath sheets flapping from clotheslines. They sidled past trash cans and huddled in holes to hide from cats. But they never stopped moving for long.

At last, paw-sore and panting, they stopped beneath a streetlight. "I think we made it," said Ishbu when he'd caught his breath. "I never saw a whisker of the Bilgewater Brigade, did you?"

"It's a miracle they didn't catch us," said Frederick. He wiped the sweat from his brow with his tail.

"Where to now?" asked Ishbu. "I'm afraid I'm lost."

Frederick sniffed the air. "This way!" he cried. "I smell stale peanut butter sandwiches and day-old Cafeteria Surprise. Come on! We have no time to lose!"

THE SECRET OF W. H. E. S.

THE MOON HAD JUST CRESTED the top of the hill as Frederick and Ishbu reached Wilberforce Harrison Elementary School. The old school building shone eerily through the fog. It stood in the center of the asphalt playground like a fortress, a ship, a castle—towering and forbidding.

Now, there was something about W. H. E. S. that Frederick and Ishbu didn't know. Mr. Stern, the principal, didn't have a clue. Even Miss Dove didn't know the secret. The Big Cheese, however, that mastermind of misery, knew it all too well.

The secret went back to the city founders— thrifty men. Some folks might even have called them penny-pinching, skinflint misers. The secret? *They built the school on top of the city's water supply cistern*—a huge underground reservoir covered with concrete— thus saving the cost of building a foundation. The cistern supplied water not only to the school, but also to much of the entire city.

The entire city! Although Frederick and Ishbu had traveled the sewers beneath the school, they had never learned this one small detail.

So the situation was even more dire than the brothers realized: water, water, everywhere, hidden underground.

Frederick scrambled up the brick wall and dropped through the boiler room window, which fortunately was still open in spite of the fog. He set off through the heater ducts with Ishbu bringing up the rear.

Miss Dove's fifth-grade classroom, at long last! Halfway around the world—from a tramp steamer, to a barrel, to a hot-air balloon, to an albatross, and now journey's end—back to Miss Dove's classroom. But were they in time?

The brothers burst inside.

"Stop!" yelled Frederick.

His voice echoed through the empty room. The children had gone home hours ago. The floors shone from the night janitor's mop. The chalkboard was blank. A single yellow rose wilted in the vase on Miss Dove's desk. No one, not even the Big Cheese, was present.

Their old cage stood on the table by the pencil sharpener, the door hanging open and a fresh bed of book pages inside as if waiting for their return. It would be so tempting to crawl inside, forget about the Big Cheese, forget about being heroes. Frederick took a deep breath.

"What now?" asked Ishbu, gasping from their long romp up the city streets.

"Dhavala told us the poison must be put into water." Frederick scratched behind his ears. "If the Big Cheese plans to test the poison tonight, he'll need water. A lot of it."

"So where does the school get its water?" Frederick continued, nibbling what was left of his toenails, deep in thought. Ishbu found a crumb of peanut butter-and-jelly sandwich the janitor had missed.

"Follow me!" Frederick sat up, his whiskers and ears alert. He set off again down the empty halls, across the polished green linoleum, staying close to the wall in case the janitor—or the Big Cheese, or any of the Bilgewater Brigade—was around.

They raced down the stairs to a long hallway in the depths of the building. A hallway filled with closed wooden doors each marked with a sign: BOILER ROOM—KEEP OUT. STORAGE ROOM—KEEP OUT. ELECTRICAL ROOM—KEEP OUT. And the last door of all: WATER SUPPLY ROOM—KEEP OUT. DANGER. DO NOT ENTER.

The door wasn't completely closed. Frederick

hooked it with his paw, as he'd seen Molly do, and it slowly creaked open. There should have been creepy music, deep organ chords swelling to a crescendo, to warn them.

But there was no sound except the screech of rusty hinges. And on that note Frederick and Ishbu crept inside.

CONFRONTATION

A FLIGHT OF STONE STEPS LED down into darkness. The brothers stared into the gloom.

"Here we go," murmured Frederick. "Buck up, Ishbu." He dashed down the twisting stairs with Ishbu a few paces behind.

At the bottom—instead of a tiny, cramped, dusty room filled with pipes and pumps, wires and widgets—they found themselves in a chamber as big as a football field and as cool and damp as the cave. A glimmer of light from a gas lantern on the floor barely lit the high ceiling. From somewhere out of sight running water gurgled.

"I thought you'd come," said a throaty voice. An immense white shape stepped out of the shadows. His head wove back and forth as he sniffed the air. In one paw he carried his cane and in the other—

—the Burmese Bandicoot!

Frederick took a step forward. A movement caught his eye—the black-faced ferret and Lieutenant Nibs. Of course the Big Cheese brought his hench-beasts with him. Who knew how many members of the Bilgewater Brigade waited in the dark?

"Welcome," said the Big Cheese. "You are just in time, my dear fellows, to see history made." He set down the statue and patted the floor with his forepaws. Finding a metal ring set into the concrete, he pulled. The lid groaned, and a hatch opened at his feet.

Water rippled below them. The Big Cheese smiled. "The water supply for the whole school. For the whole city! Look at it for me, won't you? All that clean, fresh water. Clean and fresh for now, I should say. . . ." His pointed teeth glittered like gems in the lantern light.

He pulled a small packet out of the base of the statue and held it over the open cistern.

The poison!

"Stop! No!" cried Frederick, stepping forward.

The possum's head swiveled. "Not another step, sir." His voice was cool. "Or I drop this in."

Frederick froze. "You can't do it! Think of the children!"

The Big Cheese chuckled. "I am thinking of the children," he said. "I am thinking of how they all grow up into nasty adults. Adults who shoot and trap and poison animals. What have humans ever done for animals but bring us pain?"

His milky eyes drew Frederick in. "But let's talk about you, my dear Mr. Frederick. Last time we met, you spurned my offer. I could still use such a brave, resourceful, and educated rat. What do you say now, sir? You could have fame. Riches. Adventures. All you have to do is work for me."

The Big Cheese held out the poison. The water gurgled beneath them. In the shadows, Frederick could see Lieutenant Nibs and the ferret. The wharf rat was picking his teeth.

Fame. Riches. Adventures. The thrill of sailing his little barrel-boat across the Indian Ocean. The sparkle of the gems studding the Burmese Bandicoot. The soft brush of Natasha's whiskers against his own.

"Admit it," purred the Big Cheese. "The world will be a better place without humans. Animals don't make war. Or pollution. Or garbage. We don't foul the air, the earth, the water. Think of a world without humans! All the earth a pristine and peaceful place for animalkind!" He paused. It almost seemed to Frederick that his sightless eyes glowed.

"And you could be my right-paw rat. My trusted lieutenant." The Big Cheese's voice was mellow and soothing, as compelling as a hypnotist's.

Frederick nodded. No more war. No more pollution. No one but animals, safe and secure. Forever.

"No, Freddy!" Ishbu's cry snapped Frederick out of his daze. "Who thought up geography? Latitude, who invented *that*? Not animals! And how about hot-air balloons, and sailboats, and marshmallow treats? They all came from humans, Freddy!"

Ishbu went on, his voice pleading. "And what about Martin Luther King Jr.? And Mother Theresa? And Thomas Jefferson? Yeah! Jane Goodall? And Thomas Edison?"

Frederick wiped his face with his paw. Ishbu had learned something in Miss Dove's class after all!

"Such goodness," said the Big Cheese mockingly. "What about priceless little tots like the one who tormented you—Millicent Mallory, I believe you said her name was? And then there are the dictators and warlords and criminals." He winked at the last mention.

Frederick shook his head in confusion.

"Miss Dove!" shouted Ishbu. "Remember Miss Dove!"

Like a refreshing stream of pure water, the memory of Miss Dove flooded Frederick. The spell was broken. He shook his ears and straightened his whiskers.

"Sorry," he said, "I can't accept your offer. And I can't let you use that poison!" With a powerful push of his hind legs, he leaped across the open cistern and grabbed for the packet.

Instantly he was seized by Lieutenant Nibs and the ferret. He struggled but could not get free.

The Big Cheese raised the poison again and smiled his nasty smile. "Then it's time." He turned his head toward Frederick—and since everyone knew that Frederick was the brave one, the Big Cheese didn't expect what came next.

Ishbu jumped the cistern and landed on the Big Cheese, knocking him to the ground. He grabbed the packet of deadly poison from the possum.

"Watch out!" screamed Frederick. The ferret tackled Ishbu like a linebacker. Frederick struggled to get to Ishbu, but Lieutenant Nibs's hold was too tight. It was all tangled paws, tails, teeth, and claws. In the commotion the ferret bumped the Burmese Bandicoot. The statue teetered for a moment on the edge of the hatch, then fell with a splash into the dark, swirling water of the cistern.

"No!" cried the Big Cheese.

Ishbu raised the packet of poison, and—before the ferret could grab it—he swallowed it whole.

The Big Cheese let out a roar that shook the underground room like an earthquake.

"You may have won for now, but we aren't finished yet. By gad, sir, no! We aren't finished yet!" he snarled. "Come," he told his hench-beasts. He marched blindly down the hallway, his scaly tail dragging through the dust.

Lieutenant Nibs released Frederick, kicked him hard in the side, and raced after the Big Cheese. The ferret followed. Their shadows snaked across the walls, and the sound of their paw-steps faded.

Empty. The room was empty. Except for Frederick and Ishbu.

Frederick ran to his brother, catching him just as he collapsed. They both sank to the floor. Frederick cradled Ishbu gently in his lap. Ishbu's eyes were cloudy. His breath came in gasps. His body lay slack in Frederick's arms.

"You saved them," Frederick sobbed. "Oh, Ishbu, you are the hero. You saved the children, Miss Dove, the whole city. . . ."

But Ishbu didn't answer. His eyes closed and his body went limp.

THE DEATH OF ISHBU

THE FORGOTTEN LANTERN STOOD alone on the cold concrete, casting long shadows across the floor. Through the open hatch Frederick heard water rushing along beneath the school. The air smelled dank and sour.

Ishbu was dead. Poisoned.

Tears ran down Frederick's face, dripping off his pointed nose and soaking his fur. He laid Ishbu's body tenderly on the concrete floor. He smoothed his brother's whiskers and folded his pink paws on top of his chest.

"You've made the ultimate sacrifice. You gave your life to save others. I'll make sure you have a hero's funeral, my brother," he whispered.

Frederick stood. He couldn't bring himself to look at Ishbu's body anymore. He raised his nose to the ceiling and howled. The sound of raw grief poured through the chamber. When he was empty, he hung his head, his whiskers trailing on the ground. The chamber was as silent as a tomb but for the murmur of water and the lantern's soft hiss.

Frederick closed his eyes. He put his face in his paws.

Behind him there was a noise. He raised his head, ears alert. It sounded like a burp. Where had that come from? He was now alone in the underground vault.

This time it was a loud, slow, satisfying belch. Frederick turned. Ishbu was sitting up! Ishbu was looking right at him, his eyes bright, his nose twitching. Ishbu! Not dead!

"You're alive!" Frederick rubbed Ishbu's nose with his own. "But how? You swallowed the poison! The whole packet!"

Ishbu laughed. "You know what?"

"What?" Frederick still held his brother, marveling at the warmth of the body that had been so cold moments before.

Ishbu paused, and his whiskers curled up in a ratty smile. "The poison! It doesn't work on animals, Freddy. It works only on humans!"

Frederick sat back on his haunches, stunned. He'd been so worried about the humans, and about Ishbu, that he'd forgotten. "But you collapsed! You were cold! Your eyes were closed!"

Ishbu rubbed his belly. "I have a tummy ache too," he said. "You know what? I think I'm allergic." He belched again.

"But you're alive!" Frederick clicked his teeth, and Ishbu clicked back happily.

"It's all over, Ishbu. We did it. We got rid of the poison and stopped the Big Cheese." Frederick sighed. "For now, anyway." Then he smiled. "Tell you what. Let's go back to our cage in Miss Dove's room and be regular rats again. Eating and napping, that's for us. No more adventures, Ishbu, I promise!"

Ishbu grinned. "Do you think anyone left any snacks for us?"

EPILOGUE: HOME

Home is the sailor, home from the sea,
And the hunter home from the hill.
                    —Robert Louis Stevenson

FREDERICK AND ISHBU CLIMBED INTO THEIR WAITING CAGE. After a quick snack and a drink of water, they curled up on their fresh paper, wrapped their tails around each other, and fell asleep.

So the first sight greeting Miss Dove when she arrived at school the next morning was her two long-lost rats, looking as if they'd never left.

"Where have you two been?" she asked, lightly rubbing their ears. "Never mind. I'm just so glad you're back!"

"We are too," said Frederick. "Oh, Miss Dove! We had such adventures! Travels! Explorations! Inventions! We saved the world!"

"Got any marshmallow treats?" asked Ishbu.

Of course Miss Dove didn't speak Animal, so she had no idea what they were saying. But she could tell by their friendly tooth clicks and nose rubs that

241

they were very glad to be home again.

∞

What about Millicent Mallory, Kay Serah, and Mr. Stern's plan to exterminate the rat brothers? Well . . .

Millicent Mallory's mother pulled Millicent out of W. H. E. S. and sent her to a private school, where she had a great time making everyone's life miserable. As this school didn't believe in pets in the classroom, she was reduced to annoying merely other children, teachers, and the principal.

Kay Serah tried to get her parents to send her to the same private school, but they wisely refused. Without Millicent Mallory to follow, Kay saw no point in being a bully anymore. She took up volleyball instead and soon became league champion (although she never did learn to appreciate rats).

Millicent's mother did indeed sue the school, the members of the school board, and Mr. Stern. She won a great deal of money, but the school board appealed on the grounds that Millicent Mallory was more dangerous than any rats. The case is still in the courts.

Mr. Stern got tired of the endless court battles and resigned. The school board didn't replace him but appointed Miss Dove as head teacher. She is now in charge of W. H. E. S. The first thing she did was to make sure every classroom had a pet. Or two.

W. H. E. S. is a much happier place, a blooming

place with yellow rosebushes outside and a variety of classroom animals inside—iguanas, chameleons, turtles, guinea pigs, hamsters, and rats (but no snakes).

And the Burmese Bandicoot? Is it lost for good this time, down in the dark, swirling waters of the cistern? Or will it someday reappear—as mysterious and beautiful as ever?

∞

And now, a last look at our heroes:

Ishbu curls up for a nap on the top floor of the cage. He might be dreaming of his new friends Fishbone Molly and Louie, or maybe he is just dreaming of apple cores and cookie crumbs. Frederick is down below, his nose pressed against the bars, watching, listening, learning. Miss Dove is teaching a lesson on paleontology. Frederick closes his eyes and can almost see dinosaur bones baking in the hot desert sun.

As for Frederick's promise to Ishbu that there would be no more adventures? Well . . . that's another story.

Author's Note

Frederick and Ishbu are based on two of the rats I kept in my classroom when I taught school. They never traveled around the world (as far as I know), but they did regularly escape from their cage.

Here are some of the interesting facts I learned as I researched this book:

The Remarkable Nature of Rats

Rats are found on every continent on Earth except Antarctica. They are amazingly resilient creatures, able to survive under the most stringent circumstances. A rat can—among other things—hide in a hole no bigger than a quarter, scale a brick wall, swim half a mile, tread water for up to three days, and gnaw through lead pipes and cinder blocks. Rats have been known to survive both falls from high places and being flushed down toilets.

Wild rats do indeed spread disease, damage crops, start fires, and contaminate food supplies—all of the things that I attribute to the Bilgewater Brigade. Wild rats, like other animals, may bite. If seen they should not be touched or picked up.

Tame rats make great pets. They are intelligent, affectionate, and clean. Rats for pets should be purchased from a reliable breeder or a pet store. They should be handled from birth so they become accustomed to people. As far as I know, no rats have ever built a hot-air balloon.

Bandicoots
There are two different mammals known as bandicoots—marsupials of Australia and New Guinea, and a certain type of rat found in India and Sri Lanka. The fabled Burmese Bandicoot, found only in my imagination, is modeled after the rats of India.

Karni Mata Temple
Karni Mata Temple is a real place in Deshnoke, India. Twenty thousand rats live in this Hindu temple dedicated to the rat goddess, Karni Mata. The rats are affectionately called *kabbas*, or children. Visitors remove their shoes, hoping that the rats will run over their feet, which is considered good luck. If a visitor is unlucky enough to step on a rat, he or she is expected to donate a silver or gold statue of a rat to the temple. White rats, such as Dhavala, are considered the holiest creatures. The real temple, unlike my fictional version, is attended by people, not rats.

Fire Balloon Festival of Myanmar (formerly Burma)
The Festival of Fire Balloons occurs in November

during the full moon in Myanmar and northern Laos. Paper balloons are made in the shapes of animals. A small oil lamp is inserted inside to light them and to heat the air. The illuminated paper balloons are released and drift into the night sky to welcome Buddha back from Heaven.

Australian Big Bird Race

The Australian Big Bird Race is a real race—sort of. Every year, the birds known as Shy Albatrosses make an annual migration to Africa from islands off the coast of Tasmania, a distance of nearly 9,600 km, or 6,000 miles. Some of the birds wear satellite transmitters, which allow scientists to track their progress. In recent years, people bet on which bird will finish first. Money raised from the race goes to seabird conservation programs. Albatrosses, and other seabirds, are endangered by long barbed fishing lines, called draglines.

Although Louie's trip from Tasmania to San Francisco sounds unbelievable, another seabird, the sooty shearwater, regularly migrates 39,000 miles across the Pacific Ocean from the Southern Ocean to the Pacific coast. Seabirds, including albatrosses, have been known to sail on the winds called the Roaring Forties, conserving energy for long flights by soaring on the wind currents.

Judy Cox lives with her husband and son in Ontario, Oregon. Her first novel, *The Mystery of the Burmese Bandicoot*, brings the wit and wisdom of her popular chapter books and picture books (including *Don't Be Silly, Mrs. Millie!*) to middle grade readers and draws on her own experience as a teacher.

She is currently working on the next book about Frederick and Ishbu.